UK DARK 1

THE BLACKOUT

Chris Harris

V
PRESS

VULPINE
PRESS

Copyright © Chris Harris 2022

The author's moral rights have been asserted.

All rights reserved. No part of this publication may be reproduced, stored in or introduced into a retrieval system or transmitted in any form or by any means, electronic, mechanical, photocopying, recording or otherwise without prior written permission from the publisher.

This novel is entirely a work of fiction. Names, characters, places and incidents are either the product of the author's imagination or are used fictitiously, and any resemblance to any person or persons, living or dead, is entirely coincidental. No affiliation is implied or intended to any organisation or recognisable body mentioned within.

First published by DHP Publishing in 2017
Published by Vulpine Press in the United Kingdom in 2022

ISBN: 978-1-83919-130-5

www.vulpine-press.com

CHAPTER ONE

Am I a Prepper? No of course I'm not! But then again, I like to think that being a bit prepared won't do any harm.

This is the story of how being "a bit prepared" kept me, my family and my friends alive after the world was hit by a Coronal Mass Ejection from the sun and changed forever.

The present day: Friday 9 October 2014

Becky was ahead of me, pushing a fully loaded shopping trolley and I was weighed down by four heavy carrier bags when it happened. From the High Street just behind us, came the sound of cars crashing into each other and screams. A car driving past us down the road suddenly slowed down, swerved a few times as if the driver was having trouble steering, and then crunched into a parked car. We looked at each other in horror, I told Becky to stay there and I ran back up to the main road.

It was chaos. Cars, buses and HGVs had all crashed, either into each other or into the buildings on either side of the road. I wanted to help, but I knew we had to get our children back home safely. I ran back to Becky, who was in tears. I gave her a hug and told her:

"It's going to be fine, my love, we knew this was going to happen and we are as ready as we can be to survive this. Now let's go and get the kids."

Two years previously

My name is Tom and I live in Moseley, a suburb of Birmingham, with my wife Becky, my two kids, Stanley and Daisy, and two dogs.

We have a great life; I renovate properties and sell them, and my wife, who gave up her career as a lawyer when our first child Stanley arrived, now works for a few of her old clients as a legal consultant. We have the best of both worlds; enough money coming in so that we can enjoy life without worrying about it, and the free time that you can only get when you work for yourself.

We take it in turns to drop the kids off at school and we never miss a sports match or school production. An ideal world, you might say, BUT I am an avid reader and a few years ago I went through a stage of reading disaster books, books about the world ending due to zombies, plagues, volcanos, meteor strikes, EMPs (Electro Magnetic Pulse) caused by nuclear explosions or solar activity.

You name it, I read about it. Which got me thinking, what if? Initially my thoughts confined themselves to a pub conversation with my mates. How would we survive when the zombies took over the world?

Naturally we would all turn into Rambos, heroically rescue our families and survive. Then the next day, when the hangovers had worn off, we carried on with our normal lives, forgetting all about our foolproof plans to survive the end of the world.

Sitting at home in my office one day, a bit bored and looking for something to do (other than the work I was supposed to be doing), I thought, let's see what information is out there. An hour's research later I came to the following conclusions: OK, you can discount the zombie scenario, much too "Hollywood" and totally improbable. The Plague? You either live or die, but if you live, how would you survive in the lawless empty world that would follow? Volcano?

Not many of those in England, so forget that one. Meteor strike? Well it killed the dinosaurs off; would humans be capable of surviving a decade-long winter caused by an atmosphere clogged with dust? Maybe, but then it would be about survival and I'm coming to that.

Nuclear attack? I live two miles from the centre of Birmingham, so we'd probably be toast. Nuclear EMP? That could happen, but it would only knock out the power and electronics over a specific area, so help would arrive eventually.

That narrowed it down to an EMP caused by a solar storm. There is a wealth of information out there about them, including why they happen, past events, predicted future events and the effect they would have on a modern world so dependent on technology. I discovered that a solar storm is a storm on the sun, which shoots out massive amounts of energy and particles into space.

If the Earth happened to be in the way, we would be hit by X-rays and ultraviolet light which would ionise the upper atmosphere and interfere with radio and satellite communication.

This would be closely followed by a radiation storm, which would be OK for everyone on Earth as we are protected by our atmosphere, but not so good for astronauts up in space, which is why space stations have a specially shielded area, so they can be protected until the storm passes. Following the X-rays, ultraviolet light and radiation, there would be a slower moving cloud of charged particles called a Coronal Mass Ejection or CME for short. These can cause electromagnetic fluctuations in the Earth's magnetic field which, if strong enough, can create power surges in anything electrical that is not protected.

I learned that Earth is regularly hit by these solar storms, causing no more trouble than a crackly international phone call, or resulting in their most beautiful effect, The Northern Lights, a phenomenon which most of us would love to see at least once in our lives.

I discovered that in the past, the Earth has been hit by bigger solar storms and that many have been documented, with the largest being known as the Carrington Event of 1859.

On this occasion, the Northern Lights could be seen as far south as Cuba, but more worryingly, the US telegraph system was badly affected, with operators reporting sparks leaping from their equipment and in some cases, catching fire. In that pre-electric horse-drawn era, most people were not affected. More recent events had caused power failures in Canada and Scandinavia, all short-term disruptions, because only one area had been affected, and power was quickly restored.

That didn't sound too bad and yet, sitting at my desk, I looked around thinking what would be affected if the power surge created was strong enough. The computer, full of delicate little chips and processors, would surely be damaged. My phone? Yep, basically a small computer so that would go as well, as would the calculator, printer and clock radio.

In other words, everything that required electricity in my office would only be good for the skip. I walked around the rest of my house in my head and it didn't take long to work out that anything with a plug at the end of it would probably be ruined. Looking outside at my wife's car on the drive, I realised that all modern cars have computer chips in them.

Would they still work? Another ten minutes of research left me confused, because the government agencies and scientific reports assured me that everything would be fine, and the private prepper (mainly American chat room) sites all insisted that the computer chips in cars would be fried (in other words they wouldn't!) So let's assume the worst, because would the government release information telling you that the country is not prepared for an event which would send us back to the Middle Ages?

Of course not. They'd have to adopt the attitude that it would be all right, it could never happen, and you'd have to sincerely hope that if it did, they would be in opposition government. At this point, they could stand up and blame the current government for not being ready, because had they been in power, they would, of course, have seen this coming and would have had the whole country ready.

After more research, I discovered that old cars without modern computer chips should be OK. The batteries might be ruined, but as they are much simpler beasts, with a battery to start them and an internal combustion engine to move them, they should still work. I thought about my old Land Rover (a mid-1970s model) which I used for work.

It was a great workhorse and, with my trailer, enabled me to collect all my materials from my builders' merchant for my latest project, and to take the rubbish away to the local council tip. It saved me a fortune in skip charges. Plus, it was great fun to drive, it rattled and bumped along the road, the steering seemed to have a life of its own, and the brakes always seemed to work just enough to stop it where it should, once you'd opened your eyes.

This, in my view was far more enjoyable than the modern, practical, precisely engineered cars we were used to today. In short, this was exactly the kind of vehicle I would need if the big one ever hit Earth. I had hand painted it military green and Stanley thought it looked like a real army jeep, so he loved riding around in it, pretending he was a soldier.

That got me thinking about our power supplies. Would they survive and still work? According to government papers on meetings with the power supply companies, as long as the event was not too severe, most of the power grid would be OK, as they were designed to survive the effects caused by a CME up to a certain level.

Some transformers would be damaged and power would be out over mainly rural areas for a time, until the transformers could be replaced or repaired.

I then wondered, if the event was severe enough, how many transformers would be damaged? Would the computers in the control rooms that managed the power stations and the distribution of power around the country be affected? And if vehicles were disabled, how would they even get the new spares and parts to the affected areas? And did they have spares? Presumably these things rarely broke down, so why have a yard full of spare, very expensive transformers? The permutations were mind boggling, but as I was in "doom and gloom" prepper mode, I had to assume that the power would be out for a very long time.

Is this likely to happen though, I thought? I discovered that the sun works to cycles which the scientists study and map, in order to try to predict solar activity. They all seemed to agree on a one hundred and fifty-year cycle, with the sun at present going through a quiet period, which they predicted usually preceded a time of increased activity.

The last major event had been in 1859 and as it was now 2012, it didn't take a genius to work out that we were overdue for Earth being hit by a larger than normal solar storm.

At my desk, I imagined myself turning into a caricature of a prepper, wearing a checked lumberjack shirt, sporting a big bushy beard, sitting on the rocking chair on my front porch, a shotgun laid across my lap and telling everybody to "get off ma property".

An amusing picture, but not very practical in a Birmingham suburb.

Time and life moved on, as it generally does, with work, enjoying time with the family, holidays, going out with friends, all the stuff which I'm sure we are all familiar with. The weeks and months seem to fly by with ever increasing speed the older we get. But it was always there at the back of my mind. What if this event did happen? I wasn't doing my family or myself any favours by hoping it wouldn't, because when it did, if we weren't ready for it, it would be too late.

You'd be just as stuffed as the rest of the country, for the sake of a cupboard full of cheap supermarket baked beans. So once more, in an effort to avoid working in my office, I decided to research how much food you would need to store to last a family of four for a year. The answer was a lot, not just a cupboard full of baked beans.

This is the list I made, from reading the mainly American prepper websites, in order to feed my family for 12 months:

500kg wheat
200kg rice
90kg each of beans, peas and lentils
100kg of honey or sugar
5kg salt
large tins of peppers and herbs for seasoning
150Kg dried milk
dried fruit
90kg oatmeal
loads of tins of meat, vegetables, fish and fruit

The above might seem a ridiculous amount, but when you visualise fifty-two weeks' worth of supermarket shopping trolleys, plus the last minute items you buy as extras from the shop at the top of the road, that's going to be a lot of food.

So I thought, *Yes, it's probably a good idea to prepare myself for the worst. But how will I go about doing it without being labelled the local 'nutter', with all our friends taking the mickey out of me? How will I explain it to Becky without her thinking I've lost my mind? Even telling my family about my plan will require careful consideration.*

After a long, thought filled process of about five minutes, I decided that it was best to be direct and to come straight out with my theory, then take a step back, assume the brace position and see what happened. Life sometimes surprises you.

"Why do you think this is going to happen?" she asked me.

"Right, well, it all started with me reading all those books."

"The ones I keep telling you are rubbish?"

"Yes, those. Well, that led to me doing some Internet research…"

"And that was when you were pretending to be busy in the office, I suppose?"

"Er, yes. Well, that led to further research. Just listen while I tell you what I've found out." As a result, I was now sitting across our kitchen table from her, and discussing the end of the world as we know it over a cup of coffee and some chocolate biscuits.

Over the next few weeks, Becky read one of the books, looked at the information I'd shown her and came to the same conclusion as me. It could do no harm to be a little bit prepared "just in case". I knew I had fallen in love with and married the right girl.

CHAPTER TWO

We had some choices to make. To begin with, we needed to draw up a list of items to buy and decide on the best place to go. Was it best to go out immediately and buy everything, or acquire it gradually over a period of time? The contents of the list kept changing, but the main categories stayed the same.

Food: This would obviously come first. We were accustomed to using a local trade-only warehouse for goods such as pet food and toilet rolls etc, because it was local and it was just more convenient to buy some items in bulk. We decided to buy in extra stocks whenever we went, particularly things like catering packs of flour and pasta and slabs of tinned goods. On our weekly shops, any goods we might need that were on special offer would also be purchased.

How and where should we store the goods? The garage proved to be the obvious choice. It was large, dry and easy to unload the stuff into, because you could back the car into it. The garage in our house was a huge space, built under the kitchen at the rear of the house and with a steep driveway down the side of the house for access.

I think the house, which was built in 1895, was designed to have a coach house and as the plot wasn't wide enough for a separate coach house, the architect designed it to go under the house. The garage was also equipped with a secure automatic roller door.

The tinned goods would be fine stored as they were, but foodstuffs such as pasta, rice and flour would need to be kept dry and safe from rodents. It would be an absolute waste to go to the effort of buying and storing it, only to find out that mice or rats had been nibbling away at it. It could also potentially mean the difference between life and death. Now that was a sobering thought.

Having searched the Internet and pondered the problem for a while, I found an auction house that sold anything and everything, from furniture to bankrupt stock, and at its next sale one of the lots was sealable plastic storage boxes. Talk about Karma or Cosmic Ordering or whatever you believe in, this was a stroke of luck. And who would want to buy five hundred of them? Only me apparently, and at £250 for the lot, this was an absolute bargain. As Becky had a bit of a grumble when she saw the sheer volume of plastic boxes, I decided to put most of them in the attic and bring them down only when needed. After all, it would take a long time to fill them with the goods we would be buying.

The next consideration was that there is no point in having all this food if you can't cook it. As we were living in a city, we were reliant on mains gas and I worked on the assumption that, for a while at least, the mains gas would continue to work due to pressure still in the system.

But, eventually, the gas would stop flowing. Could we cook all our food on the gas barbecue? Yes, probably. You could also buy gas bottle operated ovens for caravans and boats, so one of those would be very useful. But how much gas would I need? My gas barbecue had a testing plate on it which stated, when all the burners were on, that it consumed 1kg of gas per hour. On a rough calculation of one hour of cooking each day, I figured that a gas bottle would last thirteen days, so I would need twenty-eight bottles per year, or thirty, to be sure. That would mean storing a lot of bottles and spending a lot of money to buy them. I decided to pick up empty bottles cheap when I found them, and exchange them for full ones, but not to go mad. I therefore limited the amount to four or five, in the hope that I would find a better solution. It occurred to me that we have two log burners in our house. I'd always been able to get an unlimited supply of offcuts of timber through my work, and with the price of gas, they had helped to keep our heating bills down. If the worst happened, I was sure they would be OK to heat saucepans of food and water on.

General Equipment: This was next on the list and included candles, matches, paraffin lanterns, lighters, water purifiers etc. This was the list that you could never finish, because you were always thinking of something else you absolutely definitely needed. Again, the easiest way to buy these items was gradually, over a period of time. If you knew what was on the list, you were always keeping an eye out for bargains. I could never pass a car boot sale without popping in for a little browse.

Security: This was also on my mind. How would I protect my family and keep them safe when the social order might potentially collapse and people might want what you have out of sheer desperation or greed? Weapons. Now you're talking! I just knew the boy in me was going to enjoy buying this part of the list.

I often went clay pigeon shooting, and occasionally game shooting, with a few friends who lived out in Shropshire, so I was already in possession of a shotgun licence, and owned a Beretta Silver Pigeon over-and-under shotgun, a decent all round gun for both clay and game shooting. But was one gun enough? No. You would need at least one for everyone in the family. My children might not be old enough to handle a gun, but one day they would be, and the guns would not only serve as protection, they would also put food on the table.

I discovered that you could buy second hand shotguns for as little as two to three hundred pounds, so a trip to my local gun shop was definitely high on my list, along with enough cartridges to last forever. That was going to take some working out. Air rifles were also great for small game such as squirrels, rabbits and pigeons and under current UK law, providing they were under 12ft lb power, there were no restrictions on owning them. I didn't know much about air rifles but I was sure the gun shop could educate me.

Security also covered physically protecting the home from people breaking in. No matter how good the locks were on your door and windows, a brick through the glass would soon let them in. I was reluctant to turn my home into a prison or fort, but then I thought about the CME hitting and everything going wrong. Who cared? It was what worked that mattered. I would need to give this careful thought.

Communication: Another important item on the list. We would need to find out what was happening out there in the world and also, when it was safe to leave the house to look for supplies, it would make sense to be able to contact home. Mobile phones and televisions would obviously not be working, so that left radios for receiving news broadcasts, (if there were any), and two-way walkie-talkies so that we could communicate with each other.

I already owned a couple of walkie-talkies which had proved useful on skiing holidays for keeping in touch with the other people in my group, and saving on expensive phone calls.

A wind-up radio was also probably a good idea, as we wouldn't be reliant on batteries, which would be hard to replace. But all electrical equipment would be fried and useless. All the books I had read mentioned Faraday cages, which would protect electrical devices from a power surge. These are insulated metal boxes or cages which direct the current from the power surge around them, and therefore protect any devices inside. I decided to get or make one of them.

Fuel: I decided not to worry about that, because if every modern car was out of action, there would be plenty to syphon off from the petrol tanks of all the dead cars out there for my trusty old Land Rover (if it survived the EMP). That should also fuel the generator I had for working on houses with no power. The generator should survive the EMP because it had a simple pull-start design, with no electronics. It would be necessary to charge or power the electrical items I put in the Faraday cage.

On reflection, I decided that a few jerry cans of fuel wouldn't take up much space and I could always use it for the lawn mower and chainsaw and replace it when necessary.

The chainsaw would be essential for providing wood to keep the log burners going in the winter. It would be the only way to heat the house and provide hot water for washing and cooking when the gas ran out.

Cash: If or when the EMP hit, all electronic ways of banking would cease to work. In other words, cards would be useless. I reckoned it would be a few days before people realised what trouble we were all in, and therefore cash would still be the only way to buy goods. A couple of thousand in cash kept in the house seemed sensible.

Water: How long would the water keep flowing out of the taps? Probably not very long, as the pumping stations would be out of action straightaway. Luckily, there was a lake in the park at the bottom of our garden, which was fed by a small stream.

That could supply all the water we would need, but it would not be suitable for drinking. I'd need to investigate various ways of purifying water. A supply of bottled water was therefore essential in the short-term, but it would be too impractical to store enough water in the long-term.

Location: My thoughts turned to the holiday cottage we own in Wales. We had bought it about 15 years before when prices in that part of the country were dirt cheap. The cottage needed a lot of work doing to it, and Becky and I had had a great time going down at weekends to do the place up.

It was a three-bedroom cottage in a quiet road close to the coastal town of Barmouth. Although we'd loved going there over the years, the children's school and other commitments (such as rugby, hockey, cricket practice, classmates' parties etc) had increased, leaving few weekends free. If you're a parent I'm sure you've got the picture.

So rather than selling it, we'd chosen to rent it out as a holiday cottage and only managed to get there two or three times a year.

It would be a perfect location to run away to. It had good access to water from all the nearby streams, and potentially there would be an easy supply of food from all the sheep roaming about. Also, if you knew what to do and where to look, the seashore could provide a plentiful supply of food, from edible plants, to shellfish and not forgetting all the fish in the sea. If only I knew how to fish. As the cottage was rented out for most of the year, stocking it with what we would need would be a problem, so I rejected that idea.

We also own a towing caravan, which we use for weekends away and summer holidays when the cottage is let. A caravan would make an ideal survival home, being mobile and designed to run on either gas or electric. So technically, as long you had enough bottled gas and could keep the battery charged, it would be self-sufficient.

The electronics in it probably wouldn't survive the EMP, but everything else should work.

Becky and I discussed the "where to go" issue and decided that if the worst did happen, it would be sensible to stay at home where our supplies were stored. But if, for whatever reason, we needed to leave (for instance, if our house was no longer safe) we would need to make the best, and hopefully the right, decision at the time.

We also had discussions about who to tell and, if the event happened, who we would be able to help. We decided against telling friends or family about our plans. But if they saw all our supplies building up in the garage, what would we say then?

I had the idea of putting the crates when filled into black bin bags before stacking them with a symbol or code word on them, so that we would be able to identify what was in them when we needed them.

I would tell them they were my work tools and equipment and that Becky had made me tidy them away (not very plausible I know). If it became a problem we decided that I would partition off part of the garage with a stud wall, tell people that this was my work storage room and that way it could be kept out of sight.

Should we offer help to friends and family if they needed it? Well, if the event happened, then of course they would need it.

Food and water were going to be scarce commodities (and probably worth killing for).

My sister Jane and her family lived close by, and we always spent a fair amount of time together. Occasionally we went on holidays together and did a lot of socialising with her and her husband Michael. They have three children and as our children are all roughly the same age, it was great that they were close to their cousins and considered them to be part of our family.

Of course we would help them. How could I live with myself if something I could have done, but didn't, caused them to be harmed in any way? But we couldn't tell them about our plans, we would just have to wait and see what happened.

So, with the list complete and the planning discussed, we went back to our normal lives. Our food supplies slowly increased. I bought the equipment part of the list when I came across things. I went out and bought a few more shotguns and a cool looking air rifle with a silencer and scope.

Whenever I bought cartridges for my shotgun, I bought an extra case and put them in the store. I always kept a few 25 litre jerry cans of petrol and diesel in the garage and got into the routine of topping them up when I'd used some.

I built a Faraday cage in my garage. It was a lockable metal cage with the floor insulated with a rubber mat laid over some polystyrene insulation.

The good thing about it was that you didn't need to disguise what it was.

I would lock my power tools away in it and it just looked like a tool safe, "hidden in plain sight," as they say, so nobody would question what it was. I put a couple of car batteries in the cage, along with a wind-up radio and my walkie-talkies.

After about twelve months, the back wall of the garage was starting to look a bit ridiculous, with the bin-liner-covered storage boxes building up to become a wall in their own right. At this point I built a partition across the back of the garage with a lockable heavy-duty door on it. Again, it looked just like a secure area for me to store my tools.

When it came to the planning and storage stage Becky came into her own. She created a detailed spreadsheet with lists of everything we'd already bought and what we still needed to buy. She also prioritised them, so that the important items were never forgotten. Once every month or so, we sat down and she highlighted supplies we should concentrate on sourcing next.

Don't get me wrong, this was not a full-time job with timescales and deadlines to meet, but a five-minute chat every month or so, with Becky reminding me that cooking oil or rice were just as important (if not more so) than me popping into the local gun shop to see if there were any bargains to be had.

"Okay dear, point taken, I'll think about the boring stuff as well," was my usual reply.

As all men know, there are times when you just have to accept that your wife is right. But I would still sneak that roll of razor wire I had just bought cheap into the garage and hide it under a blanket. Then I would break the news of my fantastic purchase in a few weeks' time.

We began to keep chickens. Over the past couple of years, chickens had become the latest middle-class craze and you could buy from a range of cheap to very expensive hen houses and coops.

As long as they didn't become ill, they'd be relatively easy to look after, and the eggs would definitely taste better than from the supermarket. Stanley and Daisy, a couple of entrepreneurs in the making, set up a nice little business selling our excess eggs to the neighbours on the street.

In the meantime, Becky expanded our vegetable garden and researched and planned it so that vegetables of different types were growing and available to harvest for most of the year.

The months rolled by and buying that little bit of extra food every week and putting it in a crate in the garage became so normal it was just part of everyday life. It didn't affect what we did, or where we went, it just became what you did, part of the routine. It seemed so normal you sometimes forgot why you were doing it.

But when you looked at the partitioned off area at the back of the garage, slowly filling up with food and equipment, and thought about what might happen if it did ever did hit the fan, then yes, it had cost some money, but it was the right thing to do.

And if I was wrong, then at least we wouldn't need to go to the supermarket for dried goods for quite some time.

We created a survival file, with instructions on how to set snares and traps for animals, lists of edible wild plants, first aid advice and myriad sheets of other information that might be useful and could help to fill in any knowledge gaps we would certainly have.

I continued to read books about survival after various catastrophic events and even began to think of myself as a bit of an armchair survival expert; great on the theory, but could I do it when needed?

CHAPTER THREE

I kept an eye on the websites that gave information about solar activity in case they gave any advanced warning, but they never did.

Watching the news one night after the kids had gone to bed, something caught my attention. The usual end of the news, "light-hearted look at life" feature, designed to make you feel good after all the doom and gloom of the past half hour, was reporting on how far south the Northern Lights were going to being seen. In the next couple of days, towns and cities as far south as Manchester and Sheffield were likely to be treated to light shows most nights, as long as there was no cloud cover.

WOAH! STOP RIGHT THERE! My brain suddenly went into overdrive; Northern Lights as far south as Sheffield EVERY NIGHT! I grabbed the laptop and began searching.

All the official websites blamed it on an atmospheric anomaly that would extend the light show much further south than it would normally be seen, and in the Southern Hemisphere, much further north than usual (that's right, I forgot to mention, in the Southern Hemisphere, they are called the Southern Lights. They're exactly the same as the Northern Lights but they appear over the South Pole).

The websites were telling people to enjoy what could be a once in a lifetime opportunity to see one of nature's most spectacular displays.

I went on to the American prepper websites. They didn't tell me much either, so I went into a few of the chatrooms I'd looked at in the past.

All of them showed no activity for the past couple of days, which was very strange, as there were always discussions going on with people asking and other people answering a huge variety of questions. I then came across another chatroom and the last entry from two days ago was "GET READY HERE IT COMES!"

I sat back in my chair. I could feel my heart beating and sweat forming on my brow. It can't be happening. Why aren't we being told to get ready? What the hell is going on?

Then all at once it was obvious. Of course the government knew what was going to happen. But what could they do? You can't suddenly supply everybody in the country with enough food and supplies to last until things get back to normal. It would be logistically impossible. They would concentrate on themselves, not out of selfishness and greed, but because they would need to survive to maintain some sort of government to keep the country running and to stop the complete breakdown of society.

Telling the population would not do any good, it would just lead to mass panic. The country would have to be kept in the dark to give the authorities, hopefully, enough time to put some sort of emergency plan in place, rather than wasting their time on public order issues. A cruel and cold-hearted decision, but logically the only thing to do.

Were we ready? I didn't know. We had a garage full of supplies, we had equipment that would help make life possible and easier after the event. We had weapons so that we could put food on the table, and if it unfortunately became necessary, to protect ourselves with. We had folders full of hopefully useful survival information we could learn from. But mainly, we had the knowledge of what to expect and some sort of plan in place.

This would make us a lot better off than most of the people out there, who would soon have nothing but the food in their cupboards at home and the hope that everything would start working again soon.

How long before we were hit? That was the question that only NASA could answer. It all depended on how fast the CME was moving. They can take anything between a few hours to five or six days to reach us. NASA have satellites and all sort of gizmos pointing into space, so they should be able to work it out. But they would never tell us, because they can't. They have to keep the world's population in the dark.

So we could have hours, or days, to make our final plans. Becky had already gone to bed, so I ran upstairs and tried to wake her gently, by turning all the lights on and stripping the duvet off the bed and shouting,

"Wake up, it's happening, I told you it was bloody happening!"

OK, not very subtle, but in my defence, I was a bit "hyper" and over-excited.

Once Becky had calmed down and realised that the house was not on fire, and I had slowed my speech down so that she could at least understand what I was jabbering on about, we went down to the kitchen for a cup of tea. I explained what the news was reporting, and also the complete lack of verification from any source apart from that one warning from the American prepper chatroom site. My wife sat there, thought about it for a few minutes and then said,

"So you want me to believe, that what we have slowly planned for over the past year or so is going to happen, based on absolutely no news and only a line from a nutter on a website in America."

I stood up too quickly, knocked my tea over and was about to go on again about the Northern Lights and everything, when she held up her hand and said,

"It's OK love, I believe you. I can't actually believe it's going to happen, but I trust you. You've done a lot more research than me, and why should I doubt you?"

After a quick kiss and a long hug, we sat down and tried to find out how prepared we were. We got the spreadsheet out and went through our list of supplies. I was amazed at how it had added up over the years. We appeared to have loads of absolutely everything, but would it be enough to last? What if we had to start sharing with our family or other people? How long would it last then? The answer was who knows. More supplies wouldn't do any harm. We didn't know how long we had until the CME hit, and as nobody else in the country apart from, hopefully, a few in government, knew what was potentially going to happen, we decided that now was the time to go shopping.

We sat down and drew up a list of priorities. It covered all tinned goods, all dried goods and as much bottled water as we could get our hands on. The best place to buy this in bulk from would be the local trade-only food warehouse, but it was 11:30 at night and it didn't open until 8 a.m. That was off the destination list for now.

I went up to my office and transferred all the available money we had from all our various bank and savings accounts into my current account.

Our plan was to keep spending money on supplies until the event happened or we ran out of money. Hopefully, as I now had about forty thousand pounds in my bank account plus various credit cards, we wouldn't run out of money.

We decided we would still take the kids to school in the morning, as it was only a couple of miles from home and we could always walk to get them if they were at school when it happened. While they were at school, Becky and I would have a chance to go on the spending spree of a lifetime. We agreed that if we went out in the car we would never go more than a couple of miles from home. About six months previously I'd bought two folding bikes at a car boot sale, with the idea that, if we kept them in the boots of our cars, we would always be able to make it home.

After more discussion, I decided to start straightaway and go to the twenty-four-hour supermarket a few miles up the road. I would fill trolley after trolley with goods, until I couldn't get any more in the car. Then I would bring it back and start again. Oh well, who needed sleep anyway?

I took Becky's Volvo xc90, as I figured that, with the seats folded down, it would give me more boot space than my Land Rover. I had built some small Faraday cages for the cars, basically small metal boxes lined with rubber and wrapped in tin foil.

I put in one of our walkie-talkies and told Becky where to find the other ones in case she needed them. I also took along one of the small folding bikes.

At about one in the morning, I left the house. It was strange being out at that time of night; there was hardly a car on the road and I started imagining, *Is this what it will be like in the near future?* My next thought was, *Idiot. There won't be any electricity, so all the street lights, traffic lights and lights in people's houses and shops will be off. So no, this is not what it's going to be like. It's going to be a lot darker and scarier than this.*

The supermarket was surprisingly busy. I suppose that's why they're open twenty-four hours a day; to cater for people who work shifts, or just like shopping when it's quieter. It didn't take long to fill the first trolley full of canned food and load the car, which I'd handily been able to park near the entrance. I did six more shops before I decided I couldn't get much more in the car, and drove home to unload. Two trips later, I was knackered by the time I'd unloaded the last of the goods into the garage.

After a few hours' sleep, I woke and helped Becky get the kids up and ready for school. While she was on the school run, I sat down and wrote out the plan for the day. We'd split up; Becky would concentrate on buying from supermarkets and I'd take the Land Rover and trailer to the food warehouse and fill it as many times as I could.

When Becky got back home, she made out a basic priority list of what to concentrate on buying and off we went. It was a weird feeling; we knew what was going to happen, but couldn't tell anybody. Should we tell people? If they knew, then they could at least prepare a little bit. I'd discuss it with Becky later, but for now we needed to concentrate on helping ourselves.

On my third trip to the cash and carry I was becoming a bit self-conscious. The staff were getting a bit curious about why I was buying so much food and were starting to ask questions. Not that they minded; I was obviously spending a lot of money with them, but curiosity is only natural. I knew a few of them in passing, just to nod to and say hello when you passed them in the street or bumped into them in one of the local pubs. I made a lame excuse about a mate opening a shop, explaining that I was helping him to stock up. Bob, one of the employees, said,

"That's a bloody coincidence 'cos that bloke over there said pretty much the same thing when I asked him why he's buying more than his usual cat and dog food purchases, and he's been in at least four times today."

I looked up quickly. Just walking out of the doors ahead of me was a man, struggling with a cart fully laden with tinned goods.

As I pushed my own fully loaded cart out into the car park, I passed him packing his shopping into a people carrier which was already looking full. As I loaded up my trailer I kept glancing across. I heard his phone ring and couldn't help but overhear snippets of the conversation. He was saying he still had a few more trips to make, because he didn't think they had enough stuff yet.

"He knows! What do I do? I should go and talk to him and see if he knows more than I do. Oh well, there goes my opportunity." I watched him jump into his overloaded-looking people carrier and head for the exit. I finished loading my trailer and headed home to deliver it all before coming back for more.

About an hour later, as I was getting out of my Land Rover at the warehouse, in drove the same man. He was just behind me as I went to sign in.

"Well look here!" said the girl at the counter. "It's our two best customers of the day; you're making my manager very happy."

We both gave a half laugh, shrugged at each other and walked in to do our shopping. It wasn't that big a place; it was mainly used by small local food shops and businesses, so wherever I seemed to go in the warehouse, one or the other of us was there first, loading up similar items. I could tell he was curious as well, so I started the conversation,

"Do you happen to know something not many people know?" I asked.

"What do you mean? I'm just helping a mate stock up his shop!" he said, a bit defensively.

"I know," I replied. "I just used the same excuse when they asked me and they told me you said the same thing. Look mate, I'm not looking for any trouble, I'm just a normal bloke trying to look after my family, and if you know what I think you know, then good luck to you and I hope it all goes well for you and your family."

"How do you know I've got a family?" he asked.

"Well, call me Sherlock Holmes, but you've got a wedding ring on and half your cart is loaded with nappies and baby formula," I said smiling.

That broke the ice. He laughed, shook my hand and said: "You got me there!"

"Look, let's get on with our shopping and if you want a chat, we'll talk in the car park where no one can hear us," I replied. It took me longer to load my Land Rover and trailer, as I could get more cart loads in it, but as I left the warehouse with my last load, he was waiting for me.

"Tom," I said shaking his hand again. In response, he cringed.

"What?" I said.

"My name's Jerry!" he replied, laughing.

The niceties over with, I thought I'd better come straight to the point.

"Do you know that the Earth is going to be hit by a massive amount of energy, which is basically going to fry anything electrical and send us back to the dark ages?" I could tell my blunt description had shocked him, but he recovered.

"Yes, and going by what I've been told, we've got about three days to get ready. That's why I'm here buying as much food and supplies as I can."

"Three days? How do you know that?" was my rather shaky response. This was confirmation. Somebody knew that what I thought was going to happen, WAS going to happen. I felt a certain amount of smugness creep in, knowing that I was right and that a lot of time, effort and money had not been wasted.

"I shouldn't tell you this, but what the heck, you seem to know most of it already. My twin brother works for the Ministry of

Defence; he's quite high up in fact. He came to see me late last night, just turned up at the door unexpectedly. He's got permission, as have most of the senior officers, to tell their immediate families. This is only because they want all their officers to stay focused and not have to worry about loved ones when this Coronal Mass Ejection thing hits Earth. The sun has...excuse me, because I don't know the science behind it, or really how to explain it properly...it's been erupting with massive solar flares constantly for a couple of days.

This energy is heading straight to Earth. They reckon it's going to affect everywhere. Not one place or country will escape the effects. They can't judge exactly how much damage will be caused, because they think that even things that have been protected may not survive because of budget constraints. A lot of key places haven't been protected even up to guideline standards. And anyway, how do you know about all this?"

I explained how my interest in the subject had been aroused a few years ago and so I'd kept an eye on things. I told him about the news report on the upcoming Northern Lights phenomenon, and what the American chat room had said, and that this was why I was following the same course of action as he was. I didn't want to tell him exactly the extent of the supplies I had already collected, as I didn't know the man at all, but I do think I'm a good judge of character and he seemed OK. A bit strung out and obviously very worried, but a nice bloke.

I asked him if his brother knew exactly when the CME was going to hit us. "They're not exactly sure," he replied, "but the UK should be hit just before midday on Friday." As it was now Wednesday morning we had two and a bit days left.

He helped me load the supplies into my trailer from the cart (you see. I knew he was alright).

"How much have you managed to stock?" I asked him.

"I'm on about my fifth carload, but I don't really have a clue what the best things to get are."

"Well, by the look of what you're buying, I'd say you're on the right track. As long as the foodstuff you've bought have a long shelf life, you might get bored to tears it all, but at least you'll have food to eat. If you've only got a couple of days left to buy what you'll need for a very long time, you can't afford to be too picky and start doing meal plans; you just need to get on and buy stuff." Jerry nodded and agreed glumly.

"What do you do, Jerry?"

"I'm a GP at a practice in Balsall Heath." That interested me, because it's very close to Moseley. He went on, "I decided my family's survival was a lot more important, so I called in sick."

"Have you stocked up on medical supplies yet? They'll be an essential part of survival in the future." I asked him.

"The Health Centre I work at has a pharmacy attached to it, and as head of practice, I've got a set of keys to it. I'm planning on heading there tonight after closing time to stock up on everything I'll need."

I realised that I'd need to keep in touch with this guy. Not only was he someone who could help if one of us fell ill or got hurt, he also had a contact in the MOD, so he could be a valuable source of information on how the recovery plan was going.

"You wouldn't happen to have a walkie-talkie at home by any chance, would you?" I asked hopefully.

"Of course," came the answer, "I use it on skiing holidays to keep in touch with my mates when we get separated."

"Whereabouts do you live?" I didn't want to know exactly, as I didn't want to tell him where I lived just yet. I needed to work out if we'd be within range of each other. He lived in Kings Heath. As that was less than a mile from my house the walkie-talkies should work. He had never heard of a Faraday cage, so I told him how to build one from things he should have lying about at home and to put in any electronic devices he thought he might need in the future.

"Good to meet you, Jerry. Set the walkie-talkie to channel 2-2 tonight and I'll try to call you at eight o'clock, to check if the radios are in range of each other."

With that, we shook hands again and jumped into our cars to continue with our shopping sprees. As I was driving home my mind was racing. We now knew when it was going to happen. Becky and I needed to stop for a minute and plan our time properly, rather than running around like headless chickens.

Planning was going to be key, so as she was the Queen of planning, I called Becky on the mobile to find out where she was. She was just about to leave home on another trip to the supermarket. I told her to wait for me as I'd be home in five minutes.

At home, the garage was in chaos. We were unloading as quickly as we could in order to head out again, so mixed piles of food were just stacking up all over the place. Becky was beginning to fret about this and wanted it kept tidy so that we could update our lists. I told her firmly NO! We would have plenty of time to sort the mess out later. The important thing now was to get as many supplies in as possible.

I told her about Jerry and the information he had given me. Over a quick sandwich in the kitchen we planned the next two and a bit days. We reckoned our food supplies were in good order, but acquiring more could do no harm.

Becky would concentrate on this, either going to the food warehouse or the supermarket, depending on what was needed.

I went through our equipment list. Once again, we seemed to be in good shape, with enough of everything to last a good while. Gas for cooking was on the list, due to lack of storage space, as it hadn't been practical to keep as many bottles of gas as we would need.

On the way to my local builders' merchant, I phoned up the farm supply shop that supplied our chicken feed, and arranged for a delivery in the morning, on my account, of two pallets of chicken feed and one pallet of corn. I felt a bit guilty about putting it on my account, but figured that in a few days the least of their worries would be chasing me for money that they wouldn't know I owed them, because their computer system would be fried, along with all their account information.

At the builders' merchant, again on my account, I ordered all of the bottled gas they had in stock, along with a pallet of 18mm plywood, a hundred lengths of 100x47mm timber, thirty sheets of 2.2m x 1.2m weld mesh, post fix and boxes and boxes of nails, screws and hinges.

A plan had formed in my little mind and I was in my element. Becky's list went out of my head. I ordered rolls of barbed wire and razor wire and all the brackets and tying wire for them that they had in stock. I noticed a pallet of house coal by the entrance and ordered two of those as well. It was a good job one of the young sales assistants was serving me, because it was such a strange order to be delivered to my house, that anybody with an ounce of common sense would have questioned my sanity, or my motives.

Luckily all I got was a reminder that my account had just gone over its credit limit (oh well, shame about that, I thought) and a promise of a delivery first thing in the morning.

Next on my list was the gun shop. It was further than the two-mile radius from the house limit we had set ourselves, but as we now knew roughly when it was going to happen, I decided it was worth the risk. I still had the fold-up bike in the back anyway.

At the gun shop I thought, *Bugger the expense, why go for second hand guns of dubious quality when I've got my credit card with me and plenty of space on it?* I bought two new over-and-under shotguns and a semi-automatic, both 12 bore. All the guns I had were the same gauge, to keep the cartridge purchases simple. I bought another two air rifles and boxes and boxes of cartridges and pellets for both. In the clothing section of the shop I bought the whole family some heavy duty fully waterproof coats and trousers and some good quality boots. I went a few sizes too big with the kids' boots, figuring that they would grow into them and wear extra socks in the meantime. A few good quality knives also went into the bag. The shop owner was happy because I didn't even try to negotiate a discount on the strength of the huge amount I'd bought. As I drove home I smiled to myself, thinking, *That's the best fun I've had spending six grand in ages,* but it was time to get serious again now.

On the way home I decided I still had enough space in the Land Rover to stop at a supermarket and fill up with a few trolleys of tinned goods.

While I'd been out, Becky had managed another two trips to the warehouse. Due to our random stacking in the garage, it was now impossible to get anything else in there. We started to pile up all the new items in the kids' playroom in the cellar, trying to be a bit more orderly this time, and stacking the same items together to make it easier to sort later. Once again Becky was right, it didn't take much longer to stack it in order, but it certainly helped when it came to itemising them. As she's always said, in our relationship she is order and I am chaos.

Becky left to do the school run. This left me enough time to fit in another run to the warehouse before it closed.

Walking down the alleys, I noticed that some of the racks were looking a bit empty.

Oh well, I thought, *it's the end of the day and they might not start refilling the shelves until the staff come back in the morning. Not the way I'd do it, but then I've never run a food warehouse.* I saw the manager walking past and stopped him to ask if there were any more slabs of tinned tuna in the back storeroom, as I was looking at an empty space in the pallet racking where it was usually kept.

"I'm sorry, I really don't know when they'll be in," he replied.

"We've only had one delivery in today and that was first thing, and now I've been told by head office that all deliveries to this store have been sent elsewhere." I could have asked more questions, but it seemed pointless, the poor chap was only going on what he'd been told. He didn't have a clue what was going on.

I suspected that the same story was being repeated all over the country. There must be a government protocol to protect the country's food supplies in case of an emergency. They were probably re-routing it all to preselected destinations where the army or police or whoever would be able to guard them, and hopefully get them to people who needed them.

Muscles aching, I filled up the Land Rover and trailer and headed home. Becky and I had already decided that as we would probably be too exhausted to cook at the end of these days of preparation, we would go out and eat at one of the local restaurants with the kids every night until the "thing" as I was beginning to call it, hit.

We certainly wouldn't be able to go out afterwards, so we decided to enjoy the last two normal evenings we had left. We had a great time with Stanley and Daisy, with only the occasional glance between Becky and me, glances full of worry and emotion.

Stanley had chosen his favourite curry house for tonight's meal, and we promised Daisy we would go to her favourite Chinese restaurant tomorrow night.

After the kids settled down to sleep, Becky and I had another meeting across the kitchen table. One thing was clear, we had enough supplies to last us a very long time. As we probably had about a day and a half left we needed to decide what we should do next.

I had been thinking about this for most of the day. I felt that we had a moral obligation, now that we had enough to eat, to try to warn as many of our family and friends as possible. At least then they could prepare themselves, either by stocking up with as much food as they could or by going to stay with a friend or relative in the country, where food might be easier to obtain if you knew how to live off the land.

One thing we decided we definitely wouldn't do, was tell people how much food and equipment we had stored.

It would be up to us if we decided to help people and we wanted to avoid any awkward and probably confrontational situations, in which we would have to refuse people help if they knew how much we had. After all, they'd had access to exactly the same information as me, so they could have drawn the same conclusions and spent the last two years preparing for this to happen.

But no, they had decided to ignore it and carry on blindly with their lives.

But I do have a conscience and it would take a very cold-hearted person to refuse any help at all to someone you knew when they desperately needed it. That situation, if and when it arose, would just have to be handled very carefully, so as not to expose my family and me to any danger.

CHAPTER FOUR

The next day, Thursday, 9 October 2014 and the day before the event, would be our last full day of preparation. Becky would carry on buying from supermarkets and I, after waiting for the deliveries I had ordered to arrive, would buy some more jerry cans and fill them with diesel for my car, and petrol for the generator, before trying a few more warehouse runs. When we got the supplies home we would allocate half of them to a "food bank" that we would be prepared to give to people if the need arose.

At eight o'clock the night before, I called Jerry on channel 2-2 of my walkie-talkie. He replied immediately. Great! We were in range. He had had a good day supply gathering and now had what he considered to be sufficient provisions. He had also visited his medical practice and raided the pharmacy for all the supplies he thought he'd need to cover most medical emergencies.

He was going to spend all night, or as long as he could stay awake, going to twenty-four-hour supermarkets to keep building up his supplies. He'd built a Faraday cage and, having checked it out on the Internet, was fairly confident that it would be up to the job.

We agreed that after the event, we would leave our radios on for an hour after sundown every day, so that we could contact each other if either of us wanted, or needed to. On his travels that day he had bought a solar charger for charging the batteries on his walkie-talkies. I told him I had quite a few of those in my Faraday cage and had tried them out and they worked well. As we both still had lots to do we wished each other luck and signed off.

My next task was to start contacting my family and friends. I couldn't beat about the bush with them; I just didn't have the time, they would have to believe me and work with me on it. I wasn't going to waste my breath pleading with them. I had to hope that they would trust me enough to listen and take note of what I was trying to tell them.

Jane, my sister, listened to what I had to say, but I could tell she didn't believe it. In any case, they were leaving for their school family camping trip first thing in the morning to spend a long weekend in Wales. It was far too inconvenient a time for me to be telling them that the end of the world as they knew it was about to happen. It would just have to happen without them! Bloody family! At least I got her to promise to take their bikes with them. And who goes camping in October anyway? I just hoped that I would see her again.

It was so frustrating. Everyone I phoned seemed to understand what I was on about. But they couldn't comprehend what the future would be like after Friday. They all seemed to assume that the government would have a master plan so why was I panicking? OK, they would pop to the shops tomorrow to buy some stuff if it made me feel better, but surely it would all be sorted by Monday.

I couldn't take it anymore, so after the tenth pointless phone call, I told Becky that I wasn't going to call anyone else. They were all my friends and I loved them, but they were all too stupid to take notice and listen and I couldn't afford to waste any more time on it.

"I am so sorry, my friends. I really did try to warn you as soon as I could, but you just wouldn't listen. I only wish you had, then perhaps more of you would have survived."

The night was filled with supermarket trips. I bought everything and anything I thought would be sensible. I spotted a few other people with fuller trolleys than normal, shopping with purpose and rushing quietly around the supermarkets. Maybe word was getting around after all.

The shelves in the supermarkets were becoming emptier as well. When I questioned staff members about it, they all said that the deliveries had been delayed and that it would all be sorted by tomorrow.

I felt as if I was in some parallel universe, where I was the only one who could see what was going to happen and no matter how obvious it was, nobody understood. I wanted to scream at them, telling them to get ready, that it was the only way anyone would survive. But I didn't. They wouldn't have understood and it was too late, the food was already running out. Damn, I was tired!

After another night of only a few hours' sleep, we prepared ourselves for the final full day. Becky took the kids to school and did a supermarket trip on the way back, while I waited in for the deliveries from the builders' merchant and the farm supply shop. They both arrived before nine o'clock, so the next few hours were taken up with carrying everything into the back garden. I just covered them with a tarpaulin to keep them hidden and dry. I'd sort them out later.

I had a sudden panic. I'd forgotten something vital. What was it? Come on, I must remember. I got the spreadsheet out and carefully scrutinised it, but everything seemed in order.

It hadn't been updated with all the recent supplies we'd bought, but that wasn't it. Then it occurred to me; the Faraday cage! Yes, I needed to put everything in it and put another layer of mesh around it just in case.

I'd also decided to wrap it all in aluminium foil because I was worried about how it would perform, given what Jerry's brother had told him.

I emptied the Faraday cage so that I could re-stack it neatly and put the things I thought I would need first to the front. I collected all the kids' tablet computers, game machines and music players from around the house and put them in. Boredom would be a problem in the future if we were going to be stuck in the house for long periods of time, so even though Becky and I hated the kids' reliance on tablet computers for their entertainment, they would be great in the short term, until we could wean them off them and get them to start using their brains to entertain themselves.

I had brought the television home from the caravan after our last trip away in it. It worked on both 240v and 12v, so I could run it off a car battery. It had a built-in DVD player, so we could use it to watch films from the large collection we had amassed over the years in the house. Our e-readers went in next; we had each filled them to capacity with downloaded books. Next came the generator and all my power tools, both corded and cordless with all the spare batteries and chargers I had.

In went the car batteries with a few spare car parts such as solenoids and alternators.

I'm not much of a mechanic, but the Land Rover was quite a simple beast, and I was confident I knew enough to be able to tinker with it and keep it going with my trusty Haynes manual to help and guide me. Lastly, in went the walkie-talkies and solar chargers. I'd acquired a few more over the years so I now had four pairs still in their boxes and a variety of solar chargers of all sizes from small, individual devices to large 100w plus ones, which I could use to recharge car batteries.

Finally, I wrapped the whole cage in another layer of chicken wire and covered it with aluminium foil, until it looked like something out of a cheap science fiction movie. Looking at it, I hoped I'd understood the principles of how the cage worked and built it right. Nothing I could do about it now though, only time and an EMP would tell.

After a quick sandwich I set off for the warehouse again. Just as I was about to pull off the drive Becky returned with another carload from the supermarket and said it was getting a bit worrying. The shelves were looking emptier and people were starting to argue over the remaining items on them. The staff were doing their best to mediate, telling customers that more goods were expected any minute, so not to panic, there would still be enough for everyone. But the situation could only get worse.

I told Becky to try one more supermarket run, but not to get involved in any arguments. If someone wanted what she was taking off the shelf, or even took something from her trolley, she was to give it to them.

We had enough already, so their need would be greater than ours. I told her to be careful how she parked the car in the car park. To try to make sure that the boot was facing away from people so that they couldn't see how much stuff she had inside.

At the warehouse I spotted Jerry loading what looked like his last trolley into his already overloaded car. I walked over to help him load and to catch up. He seemed happy to see me and told me he was trying to get as many runs in today as possible, but that the shelves were getting a bit bare in there. Choice was becoming limited, but there was still enough to make it worthwhile coming down.

A mystery package had been delivered by his brother the previous night. At about 10 p.m. his doorbell had rung and outside had stood a corporal and an army Land Rover.

He'd been ordered to deliver a package to this address by Colonel Moore. It was a large metal trunk and he hadn't had a chance to look inside it yet, as it was locked and he didn't have the key. He had just left it in the garage to sort out later. He told me he thought there was evidence that local authorities knew about it now.

"A colleague of mine who works at the hospital called me on my mobile earlier. He asked if I was aware that a lot of patients, some of them his, were suddenly being discharged from the hospital by senior consultants even though, in his opinion, they weren't ready to go home yet. He asked me if there had there been some change in policy that he should be aware of.

When my friend asked one of the consultants what was going on, he looked as upset as him, apparently, but he told him that an order had appeared to come from higher up than hospital management, to clear as many beds as possible. I felt guilty for not telling him anything.

I just told him I'd make some enquiries. But it's obvious that the news is spreading and that hospitals just want to clear as many people out as they can, so that they can concentrate their resources where they'll be needed most."

The news was spreading. How long would it be before panic set in? It would go downhill very quickly after that.

"Jerry, I think it's best to get as many supplies in today as possible, because as the news gets out, things might start to get ugly. As soon as you think you've got enough supplies, the best course of action will be to lock your door, keep quiet about what you've got, and wait. You and I will keep in contact via the walkie-talkies and keep each other informed and if necessary, try to help each other."

With that, we shook hands, he drove home and I went into the warehouse. Jerry had not been exaggerating. The shelves were starting to look very empty and there were a few frustrated shop owners complaining loudly to the poor manager.

How were they meant to run their businesses when his warehouse couldn't even keep basic food stuff on the shelf? I got on with loading my cart with what was available.

I considered it my duty to get as much as possible, because now we had come up with our food bank idea, I knew that what I was collecting could be a huge help to our friends and neighbours.

I managed to fit in two more runs to the warehouse before the end of the day and stacked everything as neatly as I could in the playroom, allocating half of it to a separate area which would be our food bank. Becky had become alarmed at a supermarket when she witnessed two young mothers having an actual fight over a pack of nappies. She had then changed her plan and started visiting the smaller independent food shops in the area. It took a bit longer, just a basket at a time, but she still managed to fill the car.

She had also been to a clothes shop at a local retail park and bought piles of clothes in all different sizes, so our children would have enough clothes to last them over the years as they grew.

We were not in the mood, as both Becky and I were shattered, but we had promised the kids a Chinese meal. We put on our happy faces and walked up the road for dinner. Walking past the local supermarket, we could see long queues at the tills and frustrated customers arguing with harassed staff about the long queues and the empty shelves. Although they might not have a clue what was going on, people seemed to see empty shelves, go into panic mode and start buying whatever they could for themselves.

It always happened when heavy snow was forecast; the public would panic and start buying weeks' worth of food in case they were snowed in. In reality of course, it only snowed for a day or so and the shops might get their deliveries late due to the road conditions, but they were always open and there was always food to be bought.

I'd always had to have a go at Becky about how much food she bought for Christmas when the shops were only closed for a day. I'd never won that argument either.

We had a great meal. We ordered all our favourite starters and main courses. Becky and I shared a lovely bottle of wine and I had a couple of pints of imported Chinese lager as well. I was quite happy and slightly drunk as I carried the doggy bag home, full of enough leftovers to feed us the following night as well.

That was one less meal to worry about. Only the rest of our lives to sort out now.

After a few cups of strong coffee to wake me and sober me up I decided that I may as well try another supermarket run. I wouldn't sleep anyway so why not? I would rather be doing something positive, than sitting and worrying at home about what was going to happen. As it turned out it was reasonably uneventful; yes, there were empty shelves at the supermarket, but there was still enough there to fill Becky's car.

The cynic in me reasoned that people only panicked in the daytime and as soon as it got dark, they preferred to sit and watch TV and moan about how little the supermarket had in, rather than get off their complacent arses and do anything about it. Their loss, my gain.

When I got home, I backed the car into the entrance to the garage and closed the electric garage door. ELECTRIC, OH NO! Where the heck was that winder rod thing I used when the electric motor broke?

After unloading all the goods I'd just purchased into the playroom I went to find Becky. She hadn't been able to sleep so we sat at the kitchen table and went through our lists again, just in case there was anything we'd missed, or needed more of. We couldn't find anything amiss, although more food wouldn't hurt.

We couldn't begin to work out how much we'd bought over the last couple of days, but looking at the sheer volume in our garage and in the kids' playroom, it must have been years and years' worth.

Adding that to what we already had in storage, we concluded that we were very well set up in the food and equipment department. I did a quick check on my bank account and worked out that we must have spent over twenty-five thousand pounds on food and extra sundry supplies over the past couple of days. What a spending spree! But then by tomorrow night money would be worthless, so who cared.

We debated for a long time over whether to send the children to school in the morning. The school was only a mile or so away, so as soon as it hit, we could be there in about ten minutes of walking. Would they be in danger? The electricity would be off, so lessons would stop, but knowing the school, they would probably either continue to teach in the darkened classrooms and try to make it exciting and adventurous for the pupils, or take the lessons outside and do some "al fresco" teaching.

It was a great school and their traditional attitude and excellent teaching standards had encouraged us to send our children there.

Becky had paid close attention to the ten o'clock news to see what was happening in the world. There was no news at all about the lack of deliveries to supermarkets, which was strange because that should at least have been a feature on the local news, following the main news. The main news item was the announcement of a national strike by air traffic controllers starting in the morning, so all flights out of the country would be grounded and no flights would be able to land. The aviation authorities were recommending that people cancel plans to go to the airport in the morning, and contact the relevant airline to find out when flights were due to begin again. *Clever,* I thought, *somebody has at least had the conscience to stop anybody being in the air when it hits and has therefore prevented many thousands of deaths when the aeroplanes, as people predicted, would have fallen out of the skies.*

We decided to risk it and take them to school in the morning. It would probably be the last time they would see most of their friends, and if we went to collect them as soon as the CME hit, we should easily get them home within half an hour. In that time most people wouldn't have grasped what was happening and why their car, phone, digital watch – everything – had stopped working. There would probably be a lot of other people walking home. We went off to bed to try to get some sleep before the big day.

CHAPTER FIVE

Friday, 10 October 2014

The day started as normally as possible. Becky and I got Stanley and Daisy up, fed them breakfast and got their school uniforms ready for them to put on for their last day at school, probably forever.

We both took the children to school, as I didn't want us to be too far away from each other today. We didn't know exactly when it was going to hit. Dropping them at the school gate, I hugged them both and told them that something exciting might happen today and that if it did, they weren't to panic, everything would be OK and mummy and daddy would come and get them straightaway. They looked at me strangely with the usual "Dad's gone a bit mad again" expression on their beautiful faces, then spotted their friends and ran off to get some playtime in before their "boring" classes started. We spent a few minutes chatting to other parents at the school gate and then went home.

On the way we stopped at the garage so that I could refill the car and buy and fill as many fuel cans as they had on the shelf. The garage had the usual small shop inside so we also bought all the non-perishable items they had left.

At home, once I had unloaded the fuel cans and bags of food, I repositioned the cars on the drive so that the Land Rover wouldn't be blocked by Becky's car. Then I backed the Land Rover into the garage area to hide it out of the way. Becky walked up to the supermarket at the top of the road to see if there was anything left worth buying.

I decided to remove the car batteries from the Land Rover and Becky's Volvo and put them into the Faraday cage as well. Why not? If I didn't, they were going to be rendered useless in the next few hours, so I may as well try to save them. It was a bit of a pain unwrapping the aluminium foil and chicken wire from around the cage, but I could only blame myself for not thinking of it before. Then again, I'd had quite a lot on my mind over the last few days, so I didn't feel too stupid.

I had to laugh as Becky returned, pushing a supermarket trolley down the road with the wobbliest wheel you've ever seen. I told her she was starting to look like the local tramp. The telling off I received suggested that today was probably not the best day for bad jokes. She'd had to take the trolley as she'd bought too much to carry home and the staff seemed to have bigger things to worry about than stopping her from pushing one of their trolleys out of the door and down the road. The shelves were really empty now, but if you weren't too picky about the goods you wanted, there was still some stuff there.

I decided that we would try a few more trips together and that if the trolley was full I would carry a few extra bags. I wanted to see how empty the shelves were for myself and to get her a better trolley.

She was right. It was chaos in there. The place was full of angry customers and very stressed looking staff who were trying to calm them down. But if you kept your head down and looked carefully, there were still enough goods to be had.

People were so stupid; if the store had run out of Heinz baked beans, they didn't seem to think supermarket own brand baked beans were good enough. We filled the trolley and headed out of the door for the short walk home.

Becky was ahead of me, pushing a fully loaded shopping trolley, and I was weighed down by four heavy carrier bags when it happened. From the High Street just behind us, came the sound of cars crashing into each other and screams. A car driving past us down the road suddenly slowed down, swerved a few times as if the driver was having trouble steering and then crunched into a parked car. We looked at each other in horror, I told Becky to stay there and I ran back up to the main road. It was chaos. Cars, buses and HGVs had all crashed, either into each other or into the buildings on either side of the road. I wanted to help, but I knew we had to get our children back home safely. I ran back to Becky who was in tears. I gave her a hug and told her,

"It's going to be fine my love, we knew this was going to happen and we are as ready as we can be to survive this. Now let's go and get the kids."

"Should we go and see if we can help anyone up on the High Street? People could be hurt." Becky asked. Typical of her to think of others even at a time like this.

"No, we must go and get Stanley and Daisy first, they're our priority and anyway darling, there should be loads of people up there to help, we'll only be getting in the way."

We ignored a man standing beside his crashed car, looking at his mobile phone and wondering why it wasn't working, and rushed home to get ready to collect our children from school. While Becky quickly packed a rucksack with some drinks and snacks, I ran down to the garage, ripped the foil and mesh off the Faraday cage and opened it. I grabbed the first thing I could out of it, my e-reader, and turned it on. IT WORKED! *Yes! I'm a genius,* I thought.

I ran up into the house to tell Becky the good news, put the rucksack on my back and we left to collect Stanley and Daisy.

It was a strange walk. It was very quiet without the usual traffic noise, which you can never normally escape from in a city. The roads were full of stopped cars; quite a few had crashed into each other, but there didn't seem to be any serious injuries.

People were just milling about, looking in a bewildered fashion at their now useless mobile phones, while others had the bonnets up on their cars and were trying to work out why they'd suddenly stopped. Many people asked if they could borrow our phones as their own phones had stopped working. The only thing to do was to say "Sorry, our phones aren't working either," and keep walking.

After a brisk ten-minute walk we arrived at the school. Everything was normal and the school secretary apologised about the lights being out.

"The maintenance man is trying to fix it." She complained that she would have phoned the supply company, but the phone had stopped working as well. She looked a bit baffled when we said we were there to collect Stanley and Daisy. It occurred to me then that it was wrong not to tell these good people what was happening. The children in the school were their responsibility, and even though most parents lived and worked locally, and would be able to walk there and collect their children, some would find it difficult, as they would be stranded, possibly a long way away. The school needed to be aware of what had happened, so that at least they could plan what to do.

I asked to see the headmaster immediately regarding a very urgent matter. Why do you always feel nervous sitting in a chair in front of a headmaster? Is it me or do you always feel you are in some sort of trouble?

Becky and I told him everything we knew. We explained what had happened and what the consequences were.

He asked a few questions, but he obviously understood the main points we were making. He admitted to having read some fictional books about it on holiday last year, so it didn't take much to make him believe that fiction had actually turned into fact. I asked what he was planning to do and he sat quietly at his desk for a minute, leaning back with his eyes closed.

He responded that, obviously, he needed to make sure all his pupils and staff were safe. He could see that some of the children would be stuck at school for a while until their parents could collect them. He knew that some of the parents would be unable to collect them if they were stranded a long way away. He would either have to keep them at school with him, or see if they were prepared to go home with one of their friends. The school had a lot of food in stock, as it obviously prepared a lot of meals in one day and if there were only a few of them, the food would certainly last quite some time. *What a selfless man,* I thought, *he's far more concerned about the welfare of his 'charges' than he is about himself. An example to us all.*

We agreed that it would be best if he told every parent what was going on when they eventually collected their children. It would be up to them if they took the information seriously, and hopefully took what steps they could to give themselves a chance to survive. Becky and I were a bit emotional when we collected Stanley and Daisy from their classrooms, said goodbye to the headmaster and wished him luck. Another part of normal life, going to school, was now probably a thing of the past. What would the future hold for us?

Walking home, we told the children what had happened and why so many cars were stuck in the middle of the roads, and why people were walking around in confusion, still trying to get their phones to work, with baffled looks on their faces. They accepted what we told them in that matter-of-fact way that children have, and reacted with great excitement when we told them that they weren't going to be able to go back to school for the foreseeable future.

They were disappointed, though, when we told them it would be hard for them to see their friends.

When we arrived home, I showed Stanley and Daisy all the supplies we had gathered in the last couple of days, and also what we had already collected over the past year or so. I couldn't emphasise enough times the importance of not telling people how much stuff we actually had. I really had to get that message home to them.

Stanley was very excited about all the guns I had and wanted to start cleaning them immediately. I'd started introducing guns to the children over the past couple of years, mainly to get them used to them and to start teaching them the basics of gun safety. Always check a gun is not loaded and therefore safe when it is handed to you, and never point a gun at anyone either loaded or unloaded.

One of the jobs they enjoyed was helping me clean my shotgun after I'd used it. I'm a firm believer in introducing children to firearms in a controlled, closely supervised and safe manner. That way, they'll fully understand how dangerous they can be in the wrong hands, and it also takes some of the mysticism away from them.

They'll understand them and know how to handle a firearm safely and responsibly, if and when they are allowed to hold, or in the future, own one.

CHAPTER SIX

The rest of the day passed quietly. I unpacked the Faraday cage and brought the items needed into the house, then I reconnected the battery to my Land Rover. I held my breath and crossed my fingers when I turned the key in the ignition and said a silent prayer when it started first time. Yes! We still had transport.

We roped the kids into helping us sort out the mountains of supplies that had collected in various rooms around the house. I cleared a path to the partitioned off area at the back of the garage that I had built to hide our initial supplies when the quantity had become too much to explain away. Those supplies were the oldest, so logically, it made sense to start using them first. It was a mammoth task and it was going to take us weeks to carefully unpack and separate it all. Becky would then have to catalogue it so that we could keep track of supplies used and easily find out what we had left.

But what else did we have to do? We figured we might as well fill our days productively, if only to keep the boredom away.

After a few hours of hard work for all of us, I decided that we'd done enough for the day. We let Stanley and Daisy have some iPad time as a reward for helping us, and Becky sorted out what we were going to have for dinner to go with our left-over Chinese from the previous night.

In the meantime, I walked up to the High Street to see what was happening.

It was like a scene from a movie in which the refugees are escaping ahead of an invading enemy, but instead of a rabble of poorly dressed locals pushing handcarts piled high with their worldly possessions, the refugees were well dressed people in business suits and dresses, carrying handbags and briefcases. Even though there were no cars, people still kept to the pavements out of habit, so all the cyclists had to avoid were the cars littering the road.

Clearly these were the thousands of office workers making their weary way home. The pub on the corner was doing a roaring trade, with all the thirsty, tired people stopping off for some refreshment on their way home. The Landlord, never one to miss an opportunity, had a table outside with a member of staff selling bottles of water and crisps and chocolate bars to those who didn't want to stop. Most of the shops, including the supermarket, had closed and pulled their shutters down with handwritten signs on them saying, "Closed due to power cut. Back open tomorrow". A couple of policemen were out on foot patrol, either by choice, or perhaps because their car wasn't working either. They were besieged by pedestrians asking what was going on, and why. There was nothing to gain by hanging about on the High Street, so I went home to spend time with the family.

Getting Stanley and Daisy used to the idea that our lives had changed forever and were going to be a bit harder, was going to be a long process.

Slowly drip feeding them information was probably the best way. Kids normally adjust better to change than adults, so we would just have to see how it went and take it one day at a time.

We had a great evening. We made an adventure of it, eating our meal by candlelight and telling them stories about how we remembered the power cuts of the 1970s due to the miners' strikes. We explained that this was similar and told them about how we'd entertained ourselves.

The one thing the government hadn't lied about was the Northern Lights. We had the most spectacular light show and we sat out on the patio with the kids for hours, just admiring the beauty of it. Recorded accounts of the Carrington event had reported that you could read outside at night by the light emitted by the Northern

Lights and I'm sure we could have done the same. We sat there in awe of what we were seeing.

The kids were shattered by the time we decided to put them to bed, so after a quick story they went straight to sleep. We gave them both a torch in case they needed to go to the toilet in the night.

Becky and I decided to turn in as well. We were absolutely exhausted after the couple of days we had had. It didn't take us long to drop off.

The morning, apart from the fact that the lights and the television weren't working, could have been almost normal. Our hot water tank was very well insulated, so the water was still hot enough for us to enjoy one last shower and to bath the kids.

As I stood heating up a pan of water on the hob, to top up the hot water in the bath for the kids so that they could stay in the bath a bit longer (the hot water was now getting cold), another thought struck me. WATER!

We had plenty of bottled water to drink and a clever water filtration device that looked like a compact cylinder vacuum cleaner.

You put one hose into whatever water you wanted to drink, operated the hand pump, and out of the hose at the other end, once the water had passed through a series of filters, came clean, drinkable water. It was a brilliant little gadget but the filters only lasted a certain amount of time before they needed changing. I did have a lot of spare filters, but they weren't going to last forever. I didn't know how long the water was still going to be coming out of the taps, so why not fill every sealable container we had in the house with as much water as possible for drinking, and then every saucepan, jug, or anything else that could hold water, for cooking and cleaning?

We had water butts on every downpipe on the house, which we used for watering the garden, and I had a few extra stored at the bottom of the garden.

I'd always planned to link a few together to increase the capacity so that we still had enough during dry spells in the summer but I'd never got around to it. We could use the water from those to flush the toilets and, when necessary, we could filter it for drinking. It would save a lot of leg work, hauling water up from the stream in the park and would be a simple solution to extending our water supplies. I hadn't thought of it until now.

While Becky was going through our rapidly defrosting fridges and freezers in the house, working out meal plans so that we didn't waste anything, I noticed a few neighbours out on the street chatting to each other. I decided to go and join in the gossip. Stanley and Daisy came out with me, as a few of the neighbours' children they liked to play with were out as well.

As there were no cars flying up and down the road, it made a nice change for them to be able to run around and not have to worry about traffic, and soon a game of football was underway, with an ever growing number of children joining in.

Obviously the talk was about the power cut and why their cars were not working, and the fact that even things in the house that were battery powered had broken as well. It had taken one of my neighbours five hours to walk home from work.

I played my cards close to my chest. I didn't want to give away too much information at this stage, so I nodded and agreed to the general comments, moaning a bit about how inconvenient it all was etc.

I wanted to walk up to the High Street to find out what was happening there, so I made sure the kids were OK. The game of football was in full swing, jumpers as goal posts, the lot. They were fine, so I popped into the house to tell Becky where I was going. Making sure I had some cash on me, I walked up the road pushing our "stolen" shopping trolley before me, with the intention of returning it to the supermarket. The supermarket had a sign on the window saying that it would remain closed for the duration of the power cut, for health and safety reasons.

Oh well, that means forever then, I thought. You could still see food on the shelves through the window. *How long before someone decides to start helping themselves?* was my next thought.

Most people should have food to last quite a few days in their cupboards, but when they started running out and hunger threatened, people would turn to desperate measures to feed their families.

Breaking the window of a supermarket to get some food that was just sitting there wouldn't seem much of a crime.

I continued up the road, still pushing the trolley, to try a smaller independent mini-market, because I figured the owner wouldn't be as bothered about health and safety as the bigger operators, and would see an opportunity to make some more money. It was open, but it had a big sign outside saying, "CASH ONLY. CARD MACHINE NOT WORKING".

Great, that was one thing I still had plenty of, so I decided to see what was left on the shelves. It was busier than usual and a bit darker but there was quite a lot left. The main problem was that most people were still trying to pay by card, so it was chaos at the till.

People were not getting too angry about it yet; they were probably just a bit embarrassed, as they were emptying their purses, wallets, pockets and handbags to try to scrabble enough money together to pay for at least some of what they wanted to buy. Consequently, there were a lot of trolleys and baskets stacking up around the till with goods that people were unable to pay for. The poor staff members were trying their best to keep the aisles clear and put the goods back on the shelves as quickly as possible. I filled my trolley full of goods, waited patiently for my turn, saw the look of relief on his face when he saw that I was going to pay in cash, and pushed the trolley back home.

It was turning into a bit of a party in our street. More neighbours were gathering and more kids were joining in the football match. It was a lovely sunny day, warm for the time of year, so people were gathering, and chatting away about the power cut and how they couldn't get on with their jobs around the house because nothing was working.

I went into our house to talk to Becky about what to do.

"Should we spend the day trying to gather as much food as we can? After all, half of it will be going into our 'food bank'. Should we inform our friends and neighbours of exactly what to expect in the future? Or should we just ignore it all and carry on like everybody else, having a bit of a party because there isn't much else to do?"

"Why don't we just do a bit of everything?" Becky suggested.

I told the neighbours, as I was pushing the trolley up the road, that we hadn't had a chance to do our weekly shop so I was just "popping up the road" to get what I could.

"Let's make an occasion of the day. It isn't very often that we can all get together. Why don't we have an outside 'bring and share' barbecue to use up what's defrosting in our freezers?" This idea was warmly received and people scuttled off home to see what was lurking in the bottom of their fridges and freezers.

When I returned from the shop with another trolley load, a few of my neighbours said they felt a bit guilty as they didn't have much in their fridges or freezers at the moment.

"Well, I haven't got much booze in. Why don't we take my trolley up to the mini-market so that I can buy some booze? Anyone who hasn't got much food to contribute can come along and see what's left on the shelves. So then you'll be able to add to the party food. Mind you, it's cash only at the moment." But the three neighbours that were joining me all indicated that they had enough in their wallets.

On the way I asked them how much food they had at home. They weren't sure, but the general consensus was "not much".

"Well, since we're going to the shops anyway, you might want to stock up as well. It won't do any harm," I gently suggested to them.

The mini-market was doing a roaring trade. The owner must have had a large stock room because the staff were still bringing goods out from the back and stocking the shelves. The shop owner let us "borrow" a couple of his trolleys in return for a £100 deposit, so we formed a mini convoy of four full trolleys as we walked home. Mine was half full of booze and half full of food and the other three, pushed by my neighbours, were full of food.

On the way back I again said to them, as we walked past the closed supermarket and shuttered up shops, "You know, we can't be too sure when things will start working again, so it might be a good idea to get more food in." Two of them agreed.

"Mm. Well, we are experiencing unusual times, so it won't hurt to stock up some more. Once we've emptied the trolleys, we'll go to the mini-market again," I said. Pete, the other neighbour, seemed a little embarrassed when I asked him if he was going to go to the shop again.

"Have you got enough cash?" I asked him.

"The thing is, I haven't really, no."

"Well, I'll be happy to lend you a couple of hundred quid." Initially he refused my offer, but when I reassured him that it was not a problem (I lied and said that someone had paid me in cash for a job I'd done last week, so I had quite a bit at home at the moment which I was waiting to pay into the bank), he agreed to the loan.

"But I'll pay you back as soon as the cash point's working again."

Well that'll be never! I thought, as I was handing the cash over. But if he could get food for himself and his family for at least the next couple of weeks, I wouldn't have to worry about him and feel the need to dip into our food bank. I wanted to keep quiet about that for as long as I could.

My neighbours each managed a couple more trips up to the shop, in between sitting down with the rest of the road and having a quick drink and some food from the barbecue.

Becky did one trip herself, but on her return, she took me to one side, and said quietly, "I feel guilty now about going out, because we've already got plenty of food. Why shouldn't we leave some for other people?" I thought about it and decided that half of me wanted to keep gathering as much as I could, but the other half could see her admirable point.

"Okay," I agreed, "for today at least, we won't, but if we come upon more supplies in the future, we will get them."

When the neighbours walked up the road to return the trolleys and get their £100 deposit back, they decided to spend the money on what champagne and sparkling wine was left on the shelf. Then the party really started. It was a really good day; we set tables and chairs up in the road, and the men took it in turns to cook/burn food on the barbecue. The afternoon was full of the sound of adults laughing and drinking, while the children switched between football and hide and seek, or whatever game they could think of.

At one comical moment, a local policeman walked down the road and asked us to move everything out of the way as we were obstructing the highway!

One of our neighbours, who is a barrister, put forward a highly spirited, if not slightly slurred legal argument as to why what he was asking was plainly ridiculous, and then invited him for a hotdog and a cheeky beer. Realising that he probably wouldn't win the argument, the officer conceded the point and sat down for some food.

"I've been on duty all day, I'm thirsty and getting quite hungry. The smells wafting over from that barbecue are particularly tempting," he admitted.

Once the policeman had finished his burger and was halfway through his second bottle of beer, I asked him for a quiet word. I quizzed him about the situation we were all in to see if he had any more information to give me. He clearly didn't.

"All I know is that the police station had an unusually large food delivery on Thursday, so the storeroom's full of dried food, and all leave has been cancelled. We've all been instructed to make ourselves as visible as possible and patrol the streets. We haven't been told when the power's likely to be back on, or why everything electrical, including the cars, have stopped working." I sensed he wasn't lying and was telling us what he knew, which wasn't anything more than I knew already. As he left to go back on patrol, he thanked us for the food and happily continued on his beat.

By half past six it was getting dark and the Northern Lights were beginning to show. Blankets were fetched and passed around and the children sat on their parents' laps and looked up at the night sky. It could have been a nice way to end the day, but I couldn't get it out of my mind that all these people I was sitting with, some of whom were my friends, were in complete ignorance of the situation we were all in.

Maybe I'd had one too many drinks, but I felt I had to tell them. At least then they'd be aware of the problems facing us all in the future. It seemed only fair.

I stood up, attracted everyone's attention by tapping a knife against my beer bottle, and asked if I could have an important word with at least one member of every family present a little further down the road. I didn't want the children to interrupt what I was going to say, as it was very important, so I asked if it could be adults only.

As the group gathered round me, I made sure the twenty or so adults could all see and hear me. I proceeded to tell them exactly what had happened and why. I told them about Jerry and what he had told me, missing out where I had met him, as I didn't want people to know about the supplies I had been gathering, for obvious reasons.

I was asked how I knew all this information, so I explained that my interest had been aroused by reading various books, and how this had led to the Internet research and my knowledge about EMPs caused by solar activity.

Most people expressed disbelief and voiced their objections to my theory. Becoming slightly angry, I pointed at the sky and asked them to explain the Northern Lights. That shut the disbelievers up. I couldn't answer any questions about how bad the effects had been, or how widespread, as I just didn't know. But I advised them all to try to get some more food supplies in and to be sensible with them, to make them last as long as possible. Because let's face it, nobody really knew when any help from the government would arrive.

One neighbour accused me of holding back information.

"Why didn't you tell us all about this as soon as you knew it was happening?"

"Oh for pity's sake!" I replied. "I only knew this was going to happen a few days ago, and even then I wasn't sure. I've tried to tell family and a few close friends, but none of them took me seriously, so would you have done? No, you would have thought I'd gone crazy.

At least I'm telling you now and giving you a chance to help yourself!" Most of my neighbours thanked me for telling them, and as I had obviously ruined everybody's party mood, they quietly gathered up the rest of their families, grabbed their chairs or camping tables and headed off home. A few people hung around and asked me some more questions, as I was now the neighbourhood's resident expert. I couldn't answer many of the questions.

"I just don't know. But just keep doing the same thing I'll be doing and try to gather as much food as possible." We went back to our house to put Stanley and Daisy to bed.

Once they were asleep, Becky and I sat on the sofa, the room lit by the soft glow of a single candle, and had a quiet cuddle before we went to bed. I thought about Jerry so I grabbed my walkie-talkie and tried to contact him.

He replied quickly but had little to report. He'd had a similar day with his neighbours, treating it as a sort of holiday. We signed off and promised to leave the radios on each sundown in case we needed to contact each other.

How many people around the country had done the same? How long would it be before the reality of the situation kicked in and things started to turn nasty? Not long, was the unfortunate answer.

CHAPTER SEVEN

The following morning was spent tidying up the garage and playroom so that Becky could update the spreadsheet. I'd bought an old-fashioned camping shower at a car boot sale ages ago and installed it above the bath. It was a canvas bucket with a shower head attached. You filled it with water, pulled it up on the rope, tugged the chain attached to the shower head and water came out. All I needed to do was screw a large hook to a joist above the bath and fix a cleat to the wall to hold the rope. Hygiene was going to be important to keep healthy, so keeping clean was an essential part of survival, and a hot shower would be a luxury that not many people would have. The children were intrigued by the new shower and couldn't wait to try it out. It had taken a worldwide disaster to get my children to want to have a shower. Typical!

After a lunch of fridge leftovers, Becky decided to start cooking the perishable food we had left to make it last longer.

She also went through the cupboards in the kitchen and pantry, to make sure that we weren't going to waste anything by letting it go off.

"I'm warning you now that meals might be a bit strange."

"You're a great cook, and I'm sure whatever combination you come up with will be fine with me," I reassured her.

I walked up the road to see what, if anything, was going on. I took the trolley with me in case I came across any foodstuff. As I passed a small clothes shop and the local electrical goods retailer, it was obvious they had been broken into during the night and ransacked.

It hadn't taken the local criminals long to realise that without power, burglar alarms wouldn't work, so they could easily break in undisturbed and help themselves. *So when will they pluck up the courage to break into houses with people in?* I wondered.

The mini-market was still open, but the policeman who'd joined us the previous night was standing outside, so I stopped to have a chat.

"Someone tried to break in, but they were disturbed by the owner who lives here in the flat above the shop. I'm here to be visible and to remind people to behave, after more break-ins at some of the other shops on the High Street," he told me. Inside the shop, people were still trying to buy goods with their cards and the owner was becoming less polite about refusing them. The customers were becoming angry at being refused, and cross words were being exchanged as the rejected customers left the shop, but the inbuilt British sense of right and wrong and politeness was still holding.

The situation wasn't getting out of hand just yet. The shopkeeper's prices seemed to have doubled overnight, but I didn't say a word as I filled my trolley and paid at the checkout.

The shop still had a fair amount of stock on the shelves, as most of his customers probably hadn't had enough cash to pay. I decided to keep returning and buying the food while it was still on the shelves.

The next couple of days passed quietly. Most of the time was spent sorting the supplies out and we only ventured out of the house to walk the dogs in the park and let the kids run off some energy. I began to look forward to my nightly radio chats with Jerry, and the more we talked, the more our friendship grew.

He was doing the same as us, staying in and not drawing attention to himself, and waiting to see what the future held. We were much more willing to trust each other now, and as proof of this, he told me about the crate his brother had sent him before the event. Another military Land Rover had turned up on the Thursday before the event with a smaller package containing the key and a letter from his brother.

The letter had said that he wouldn't be in touch for a long time, as his command was following protocol and had retreated to a secret secure base, along with key members of the government. They would be hiding away there until they could work out how bad the situation was, and from there they would try to coordinate the relief effort.

I had seen this in films. I suppose it's called "continuation of government," but normally in films the select few act like cowards, only look after themselves and ignore the rest of the population, while living in relative luxury. I could only hope that, as those films were normally American, the British government would have a better moral code and would want to help its people.

The crate had contained packets of MREs, pre-packed ready to eat meals (hence the name MRE: Meals Ready to Eat). I've never tried one, but apparently, they don't taste very good, although they do provide you with enough calories to keep you going.

In addition to the food, the crate had contained a military looking radio with instructions on how to use it. At the bottom of the crate there were two military rifles and two handguns, one shotgun and boxes of ammunition for all of them.

His brother had taken the weapons out of the base stores in the knowledge that in the ensuing chaos they wouldn't be missed. He'd sent the key separately to stop anyone opening the crate and discovering what he had done.

Jerry said that he'd left them in the crate and hoped he wouldn't have to use them, since he hardly knew which end of a gun to hold.

I told him that with my limited knowledge of guns, if he ever wanted help, I was sure I would be able to work them out and give him some basic instructions. We bid each other good night and signed off. *WOW,* I thought, *the guy's a doctor and has some proper military grade weapons! If we pooled our knowledge and resources we could really help each other out in the future.*

CHAPTER EIGHT

That night we had our first tragedy on the road. Nobody was able to say exactly what happened, but in the middle of the night I was woken up by a commotion outside. A house about ten doors down was ablaze. I ran out to help. A crowd of neighbours was already gathering and I shouted, "Has anybody got out?" The ground floor of the house was an inferno and there was no way in or out, so nobody thought they had. I grabbed a neighbour and told him to come with me. We ran back to mine and I shouted to him to grab my ladders so that we could reach the upper windows. I ran through the house to my garage and wound the garage door up just enough to slide my ladders out. I felt the neighbour grabbing them, so ran back through the house and out of the front door, and we carried them down the road. We tried to put the ladders up to the upstairs windows but were beaten back by the intense heat and smoke.

People had formed a bucket chain, but it took so long to fill the buckets up that it was pointless, and eventually we had to give up. Luckily, it was a detached house so the flames couldn't easily spread to neighbouring homes. We all felt helpless as we stood there and watched. Someone had seen the family earlier in the day so we knew they'd been in.

We could only guess that as candles or oil lamps were most people's only source of light, either through carelessness or sheer bad luck, something had caught fire.

A police foot patrol turned up, but as it was clear nothing could be done until the fire had burned itself out, they took the details of who was living in the house, and concluded that they were most probably dead. They gave everybody a lecture about being careful with naked flames.

A group of us agreed to stay and make sure the fire didn't spread. They apologised for not being able to do anything else and left to continue on their patrol.

As we stood around, traumatised by the night's events, a few of the neighbours admitted that they were running low on food and were planning to leave to go to friends or relatives they knew who lived out in the countryside where, hopefully, the situation was better. I asked them how far they were going to be travelling. One was going to just south of Worcester and the other to a place not far from Stafford. They all had bikes and teenage children, so were expecting to make it in a long day's ride (they were planning to bike along the motorways as they were the most direct route).

"Just remember that you can expect to see some horrific crashes on the motorways. Try to prepare your family for the sights they might see," I warned them.

Everybody was running low on food, but I didn't want to open the food bank yet, because I believed there was still probably food to be had out there, if you looked hard enough.

The situation was not desperate yet, and if two of the families in the street were planning to leave, how many more were thinking about it? This would mean there would be more food to go round when the time was right. I was not trying to play God, I was just trying to be practical with the limited supplies I had available, in order to help my friends and neighbours.

A few days later, I walked around the streets again, trying to get some idea of what was going on. The streets were quiet, but on the High Street every shop, including the supermarket, had been broken into and looted. Looking through the broken glass of the supermarket, the place had clearly been ransacked and every shelf had been stripped bare.

People are running out of food and getting desperate, I said to myself. *Now is the time to start taking home security seriously. Desperate, normally law-abiding people will be breaking in and trying to take what we have.*

Walking down the next road, I saw a crowd of youths surrounding someone. As I got closer, I saw it was an old man pulling a shopping trolley, one of those two-wheeled ones your grandma always had. They were pushing and jostling him, asking him what he had in his trolley. A few people had crossed the street, not wanting to get involved, but, being stupid, I decided I couldn't let this happen in broad daylight a few streets away from my house.

"Hey! Leave him alone!" I shouted, trying to sound as tough and authoritative as I could.

"Piss off, what are you gonna do about it?" came the reply from the one who was obviously the leader. He was a skinny eighteen-year-old lad in the classic tracksuit and baseball cap. All his clothes looked brand new, even his trainers.

Been helping yourselves from the local shops then? was my thought, but that was the least of my concerns, as they all turned their attention on me.

I'm not a small bloke and I could have handled one or two of them I suppose, but unfortunately there were five of them, not good odds at all. Luckily another man, who had initially walked past but had probably had an attack of conscience, decided to join me, saying,

"If you don't piss off right now, I'm gonna come over and rip your head off your scrawny neck and stuff it up your mate's arse!"

I looked over at him, admiring his command of the English language, and nodded in thanks. That made the youths think a bit. Two against five were clearly not such good odds for them, particularly as the man who had joined me looked as if he could follow up on his threat. He was about six foot six and looked as if he played a lot of rugby. There was a shout from further up the road and looking round, I saw a policeman jogging towards us.

The youths spotted him and decided to run away, shouting obscenities over their shoulders as they ran.

"Thanks for helping," I said, and shook his hand.

"I'm sorry I didn't stop them earlier, but I've been trying to find some food for my family, and I didn't want to get involved in anything that might stop me. But when I saw you step in, I thought I should as well." The policeman arrived out of breath. It was my barbecue friend again.

We checked that the old man was all right, which he was, and he told us he'd been on his way home from his allotment, where he'd just been harvesting some vegetables to eat. He offered me and the other man (to my regret, I never got his name) some of his vegetables as a thank you. I refused, but his other saviour was very grateful, saying that he and his family had run out of food the previous day and he was desperately trying to find some.

On hearing this the old man said, "Why don't you take all these then, I can easily get some more, and if you want to come with me up to my allotment again in the morning, in return for being my bodyguard, I can give you some more." The man was so grateful, he insisted on escorting him home. As they said goodbye I only hoped that a mutually beneficial relationship had begun.

CHAPTER NINE

The policeman and I, as we had now met a few times, introduced ourselves to each other. His name was Allan. We walked along together, and talked about the situation.

"It's getting out of hand," Allan told me. "Gangs are robbing every shop they can get into, and if the shop owners are there, they're beating them up as well. There hasn't been any official communication from central command or any of the other stations. When I've bumped into other officers from neighbouring stations, they've told me about similar scenes. Most officers have stopped reporting for duty now, because they think they need to be at home to protect their own families. I'm not married and I haven't got any family close by. I've even started to sleep at the police station, because it's got a few camp beds. It doesn't seem worthwhile going home when I'm working fifteen hours a day and all the food's at the station, while my cupboards at home are bare."

"Come on back to my house for a cup of coffee and some food," I said, and he gratefully accepted. Sitting at my kitchen table, eating bowls of soup and drinking big mugs of coffee, I asked him what the current policy would be on protecting your home and family from being robbed.

"Well, of course you can't step outside the law, but in my opinion, leniency should be given to those protecting what's theirs, as long as excessive force isn't used," I argued. "Yes, but whatever the law might state at the moment, the EMP will mean that nothing is likely to return to normal in the near future and that possibly, it might never do."

"EM what?" was his reply. I couldn't believe that nobody had told the police what was happening. They were the people who were responsible for keeping public order. What a monumental cock up that was!

I told him everything I knew, including what Jerry had told me about the government going into hiding, my predictions about the countrywide food situation, or lack of it, that most people were experiencing, and how help was unlikely to be arriving any time soon (unless the government had some amazing plan so save us all).

"Yes, but all the diverted food supplies must be stored somewhere." It was a good point, but I explained,

"No matter how carefully it's distributed, the food will only last the country a matter of days, or a week or two, at the most. It's only going to delay the inevitable starvation that will follow, and with winter approaching, the situation isn't going to get any better. People are going to start dying soon and there's nothing anybody can do about it."

Allan left to carry on his patrol and his single-handed effort to keep order in the local area. I wanted him on my side, so I offered him two of my walkie-talkies so that he and another colleague could stay in contact, and coordinate their efforts if necessary.

"If you drop them in when you're passing, I'll recharge them from my solar charger and you can pick them up later on." He was very pleased with the offer and thanked me for trying to help the community. I suppose I was, but having a police officer visiting regularly to drop off and collect the walkie-talkies would be no bad thing. And if I was seen as "the good guy", if anything happened in the future, I hoped they would automatically assume I was in the right and was only trying to do my best in difficult circumstances.

That night the gas stopped flowing. Water was still coming out of the taps, but the pressure was reducing daily and sometimes it was a bit cloudy.

I decided to stop using it for drinking, as it was likely that the treatment plants wouldn't be working and therefore you couldn't be sure if it was safe to drink anyway. I brought up the camping cooker and grill and set them up in the kitchen.

I figured we'd have enough gas to last over a year, but we may as well be careful how much we used, to make it last as long as possible.

We were fine for water, with all the water butts in the garden, the stream in the park and the means to filter it all for drinking, so I wasn't worried about that at all. We also had a good supply of bottled water. But it was going to get much more difficult for other people now.

In the morning, as we were having breakfast, there was a knock at the door. It was Pete, one of our neighbours.

"Bad news, I'm afraid. A house at the bottom of the road has been broken into overnight, while the family were asleep. They've been roughed up a little, but they're fine. But their remaining food has been stolen and I want to call a meeting of all the neighbours to see if there's anything we can do to help protect ourselves more."

Great, I thought, *this is what we need, a proactive neighbourhood watch. It will help us all.* As I was leaving my house with Pete to round up the rest of the neighbours, Allan turned up with the walkie-talkies for charging. I told him what had happened and invited him to the meeting.

We managed to bring about twenty neighbours together, half of whom lived on our road. The remainder didn't want to be involved and were not concerned about helping others. Frustrating, but understandable. But they wouldn't mind selfishly benefiting from our efforts, would they!

Mentally, I removed those people from my food bank help list. The meeting was very productive and we quickly organised a patrol rota, split into three-hour shifts, so that at least two of us would be "on duty" twenty-four hours a day.

We asked Allan how far we could go in protecting ourselves and our property from attack. He thought for a while and then said, "As of this morning, I'm now the only policeman reporting for duty in Moseley, and given what you told me only yesterday, as far as I'm concerned, I'm the only help that's going to arrive. So, in my view, you should do what you think is necessary and what your consciences will allow you to do."

That statement made us all go quiet. We were now the Law! It was like the Wild West. I just hoped it wouldn't result in hanging the bad guys from the nearest lamp posts to teach the rest a lesson. That started a very lively discussion about how far we would be prepared to go, with the liberals suggesting that a stern telling off would be sufficient to deal with the ruffians, and the more right-wing members, me included, argued.

"The only way to deal with them will be to give them a taste of their own medicine and show our strength. That will make them think twice about bothering our small community. There'll be no police cars screaming down the road with lights flashing so we're on our own."

I steered the conversation around to food in an attempt to find out how well my neighbours were coping. Most were running low, which was a concern, so I made a suggestion.

"Why don't we organize trips to all the local shops to see if any food is still available, and then we can share it out with everyone who's joined in with our efforts."

Allan said not to bother, as he had walked around all the local businesses in the last few days, including those that sell food.

"In my opinion," he told us, "not one of them has got anything left to sell, or they've closed and are saving what's left for themselves. There are still a lot of supplies left at the police station, though, even after most of the officers stole what they could to take home to their families. If you're willing to police your road, and help to keep order, then I'm willing to share the supplies from the station, once I've taken what I think I need for myself." This was a generous offer and we gratefully accepted.

I had read in a lot of survival books, how some groups had barricaded their roads to keep out trespassers. I put this forward as an idea.

Most people didn't want to do this just yet, which I understood, as it had only been a week since the EMP.

Although things were bad and there were no signs of it getting better, taking the decision to barricade ourselves in seemed a step too far at that moment.

We soon established a routine of patrolling in pairs and, apart from the shifts in the early hours of the morning, which nobody enjoyed, it seemed to give everyone a sense of purpose and worked well. The neighbourhood seemed to become closer and there was a real community spirit. Even some of the neighbours who had initially refused to help saw the benefit of what we were doing, and joined us. Pete assumed the position of leader of the neighbourhood watch, which none of us minded. He'd run a large and very successful business, so he had great people skills and was very well liked and respected on the street.

Of course, the food supplies given to us by Allan, the policeman, helped, so no one was going hungry yet. Everyone's basic needs were being met, and therefore, jealousy about what other people might have had not come into the equation. We were just mucking in together to help each other out.

I kept in regular contact with Jerry. His neighbours were not doing anything to help each other and there had been quite a few robberies on the road. A lot of them had left to try to get to friends who lived out of the city, or just anywhere where there might be some food.

He seemed exhausted, as he spent nights awake, in case someone tried to break in. He hadn't taken any of the guns out of the crate yet.

"You must," I urged him. "You need to protect yourself and your family, and because you're on your own, weapons are probably the best answer." We agreed that I would visit him, so that I could give him some basic instructions (providing I could work out how to use the guns myself).

He told me where he lived and I arranged to go round the following morning.

I told Allan, by now a daily visitor to our road, what Jerry had said.

"Yes," he confirmed, "as far as I know, you're the only road to have banded together to help each other out. The situation's getting worse by the day. Gangs are beginning to roam the streets, mugging anyone they come across and breaking into houses to steal supplies. I'm beginning to feel very vulnerable and exposed when I'm out patrolling on my own. I really don't know how much longer I'm going to be able to do it. I can't be everywhere at once and as soon as the criminals watch me leave an area, they just start again."

"Are you still carrying one of my walkie-talkies, because remember, we've already said we'll come to help you if you need us."

"Well, I think that, since no property or person in your road has been attacked, word must have got around about your patrols. For the moment, there are easier targets out there."

Bangs that sounded like gunshots were becoming daily occurrences and at any time of the day you could see a plume of smoke rising, presumably from another house on fire.

I couldn't help thinking, *Where are the people who could help, the police, the military, anyone? The only official person we've seen in the past week is Allan and he's doing his best, but he can't arrest anyone any more. There's no one else to pass the prisoners on to; all he can do to try to prevent crime is stay visible and chase the bad guys away.*

I told Allan, "I'm going to see a friend in Kings Heath tomorrow. Would you have any objection to me taking my shotgun for protection.?" I had told him early on that I was a shotgun licence holder and so I had a few guns in the house.

"Tom, do whatever you want, I'm not going to stop you. Just be bloody careful and don't do anything you'll regret."

CHAPTER TEN

In the morning, I called Jerry on the walkie-talkie and told him to expect me in about thirty minutes. I kissed Becky and the kids goodbye and promised to be careful. It felt strange to be walking up my street with a shotgun over my shoulder. (OK, I'll admit it was pretty exciting as well.) The walk was uneventful and hardly anyone was around. The High Street was a mess, with every shop and pub broken into. Peering inside the broken windows, it was plain to see that anything of use had already been stolen. A lot of houses looked empty, most with doors kicked in and windows smashed. I spotted a few people looking at me from behind windows. I waved, but no one came out to say hello. I suppose the shotgun must have had something to do with it, so I just carried on walking. I thought to myself, *How many people are left in the city and where have they all gone to? The whole place feels abandoned and it's only been just over two weeks.*

I walked past my sister's house and felt a pang of sadness, wondering where she and her family were. I hoped they were surviving. The front door had been kicked in, so I went inside. The place had been ransacked and every cupboard in the kitchen had been emptied in the search for food.

I knew Jane kept most of her food in her cellar, so I tried the door. It was still locked. The idiots had been so busy stealing my sister's now useless television, and grabbing things that were easy to find, that they hadn't done a thorough search. I would have to return later with some help to get whatever was in the cellar.

I knew Jane was in the habit of ordering a big monthly delivery from the supermarket to save shopping weekly, so potentially, there could be a lot of food stored in there. As I left the house, I took care to leave the front door open, so that it was obvious it had already been broken into, in the hope that this would deter others.

Jerry lived in a nice, detached house on the Moseley/Kings Heath border. He was looking through the front window, waiting for me to arrive, and he opened the front door as I walked up the drive. We shook hands and he introduced me to his wife, Fiona, and his two children, Larry (who was four) and Jack (who was six months old). I called Becky on my walkie-talkie to tell her I had arrived safely. Because we chatted most nights on the walkie-talkies, we didn't have lot of catching up to do, but I filled him in on what Allan had told me the previous day about the gangs and how, in the space of two short weeks, society had collapsed. I told him that things were likely to get worse the hungrier and more desperate people became.

"Someone tried to break in last night," Jerry told me, "and they ran off when I hit the first bloke, when he was trying to climb through the kitchen window. I clobbered him around the head with a cricket bat. I think there were about four or five of them. Fortunately, they were a bunch of cowards and they ran at the first sign of opposition."

"Come and stay with us, or at least in one of the abandoned houses in our road." He already knew what we were doing to protect ourselves collectively and he said, "Fiona and I discussed joining you. Until last night we still felt relatively safe in our house and I think that as long as I'm vigilant and make myself visible, no one will try to break in."

"Well, if you say so, but, please, give it some serious thought."

Then we got on with the purpose of my visit. I helped Jerry carry the crate into the lounge and he took the key out of his pocket and opened it. Lying at the bottom of the crate on top of boxes of ammunition were two Heckler and Koch MP5 sub machine guns with silencers on them, two Glock pistols in holsters and a pump-action shotgun, along with spare magazines for them.

"Bloody hell mate, you've got some serious fire power here," I whispered excitedly. "Your brother's done you a big favour. He must have some pull to be able to get these out of his base and deliver them to you."

I had to get them all out immediately just to admire and hold them.

"Right then, which one shall we play with first?" was my slightly childish question, in response to which Jerry laughed, as he could see how excited I was. As we unpacked the crate, I realised that there were only 9mm bullets and shotgun cartridges. The Glocks and the MP5s clearly needed the same ammunition. That was good news, because although I hadn't counted the bullets yet, there seemed to be a lot of them. There weren't as many shotgun cartridges, as these probably took up a lot of room, but I had plenty of those at my house anyway. I picked up the MP5 and starting loading one of the ten magazines from the crate. I had never done this before, but had seen it done in films. Once I had it fully loaded, I told Jerry to show me how to get to his back garden, which he did.

"Right then," I said, standing with the gun in one hand and the magazine in the other, "let's see how these things work." I inserted the magazine, pulled back the cocking lever and put the gun to my shoulder. I aimed at a tree in the back garden and pulled the trigger. Nothing!

"Oops," I said, "I must have forgotten the safety." Making sure the gun wasn't pointing at anybody, I looked at the side of it and saw a lever by the trigger.

I saw four positions and from the symbols by them it was easy to work out that they went from safe to single shot then to three-shot burst, then full automatic. I selected single shot and again aimed at the tree and pulled the trigger. The silencer worked well; there was just a low cracking sound and that was it. Looking at the tree, I thought I'd missed it. I selected the three-shot burst, aimed and pulled the trigger again. At least one shot hit home.

I could have played with it all day, but I was there for a reason. I showed the features on the gun to Jerry, gave him the basic gun safety rules, like how to check it was loaded and therefore ready to fire, and how the safety worked. I suppose the rule of not pointing a gun at anybody was now irrelevant, so I changed it to never pointing a gun at anybody you didn't want to shoot.

Jerry fired a few shots at the tree. *Bloody hell, he hit it more than me. But that's only because I'm such a good instructor,* I thought to myself. The Glock was a bit trickier to work out, because it didn't have a safety. If you held the gun in the correct firing position, somehow it activated the gun and you could fire it. We took a few shots each, but we didn't want the noise to attract any unwanted attention, or to waste ammunition. The shotgun was a pump-action and loaded in a similar way to my semi-automatics, but this one held eight cartridges.

I showed Jerry how it worked, but his children had been upset by the noise from the Glock, so we decided not to shoot it for now.

Back in the house, he showed me the radio that had also been in the case. It was quite a large, impressive looking military-type communication radio. We tried turning it on, and to my surprise, the lights came on. It seemed to be OK and had clearly survived the EMP. When I examined the crate, I realised why. It was made of heavy duty metal with a foam padding lining and must have been specially designed to protect its contents from the effect of an EMP. We couldn't pick anything up on the radio, so we turned it off, because we couldn't see a way of charging it and could only speculate as to why his brother had included it in the crate, along with the instructions.

We spoke again about moving to my road, so that he and his family could be safe.

"The main problem is the amount of supplies I gathered in the days before it happened, and how to move them. Look at all this I collected." It was an impressive amount, almost filling a large spare bedroom in his house.

"Mm," I said. "There's far too much to move by carrying it. The only logical way would be to get my Land Rover out of the garage, hook the trailer up and keep going back and forth until everything's moved. But I haven't told anyone on my road, not even Allan, my policeman friend, that I've got a working vehicle."

Will people think I should have told them? Will they wonder what else I didn't tell them? Will I be exposing myself and my family to more danger? Even though we're working well together as a neighbourhood, will the temptation of finding a way out of the city, to a place that might be safer, prove too much for some of them? These thoughts were running through my mind, and I had a feeling that the cooperative was only going to last as long as the food supplies did. Jerry took the conversation up.

"The car itself is going to be a massive problem as well. The noise is likely to attract unwanted attention and could lead to dangerous confrontations, because everybody will want it at any cost."

The more we talked about it, the more obvious it became that driving to and from his house was going to be completely impractical, if not potentially deadly.

We agreed it was certainly a dilemma, and fortunately, Jerry understood my position immediately.

He said if it was going to cause me trouble, he wouldn't move and would find a way to manage at his house. I wouldn't hear of it.

"If there is a way I can think of doing it, without any repercussions, then it's going to happen and that's the end of it," I told him and his wife.

"Well, I do now feel confident with the weapons and how to use them. I'm sure we'll be safe staying here until we can think of a way of moving everything without arousing unwanted suspicion."

"Jerry, have you got somewhere in the house where we can hide your supplies?" I asked. He wasn't sure, so I asked him to show me round.

His house was the typical turn of the century type, with rooms on the third floor in the eaves and no attic, so that ruled out hiding anything there. However, most old houses have a cellar, so I asked him to show it to me. It was a large cellar split into several rooms by the supporting walls in the house, with a door-sized opening between them.

With the light of the torch Jerry had provided, I could see that the first room was lined with shelves full of the normal things you would find in a cellar. The other rooms were empty and Jerry explained that he had always planned to board them out and turn them into more usable space, rather than just have the plain brick-floored and brick-lined rooms they were now.

As it was likely to involve quite a bit of work to damp-proof them properly, he hadn't got round to it yet. An idea formed in my mind.

"How about we move all your supplies into one of the back rooms in the cellar, then move one of the shelf units over the opening? That'll hide it and if people break in, they most likely won't have torches with them anyway, and all they'll be able to see is one room lined with shelves." It seemed a simple but effective solution.

"Good plan. I'll make a start moving our supplies as soon as you've gone."

Before I went, I helped him board up his broken kitchen window with a few old pieces of timber we found in his shed, and we checked for any other weak points around the house where someone could break in easily. There were a few, but without proper materials, all we could do was push tables and pile chairs against the French windows leading on to his patio to make a temporary barrier. Anything that might slow them down would give Jerry time to react.

I radioed Becky and told her I was on my way back.

As I was leaving, Jerry insisted on giving me one of the MP5s, a pistol and five hundred rounds of ammunition, saying that as there were only two people in the house who could use the weapons and he still had three left, there was no point in letting them sit there.

I have to admit that I was hoping he would, so I accepted straight away and thanked him profusely.

I'm not daft. Jerry's thoughts were transparent.

"If the neighbours in the road see the weapons you've got access to, they'll be far more amenable to letting you and your family join us." I smiled as I told him this and he looked a bit sheepish about being found out, but I laughed and said, "It's exactly what I would have done." I walked home in a hurry, because it was starting to get dark and I was due on neighbourhood patrol soon.

Later that evening, Jerry called me on the walkie-talkie. He asked me about my old Land Rover and why it was still working.

I explained about the engines in older cars being simpler and not having computer chips and that as soon as I'd changed the battery in mine, it had worked just fine.

"So let's find another old car then, and we can get it going and move all my stuff over to your road. Everybody must assume that all cars aren't working, and aren't aware that with some cars, all it'll take is a new battery. If we can find one and get it working then nobody will need to find out about yours."

"Brilliant idea mate, you are a genius!" I replied, amazed at how simple some solutions can be.

"There's someone on the next road to us who has a vintage Land Rover. In the morning, I'll take a quick trip out to see if it's still there and I'll radio you so that we can plan the next move," Jerry said, as we ended our radio chat.

That evening there were more shouts and screams and at least four gunshots that sounded close by in the local area. I'm not an expert, but it sounded like a shotgun being discharged.

I'd heard enough being fired in my time so I was confident it was. The neighbours were becoming very nervous now and the two of us in the road who owned shotguns decided, after getting the agreement of the others, that it was time to start carrying them with us, if not all the time, then at least when we were on patrol duty. I had to give Bob, the other shotgun holder, a few boxes of cartridges, as he didn't have any. That night, on patrol, I carried my semi-automatic shotgun and my Glock in its holster, hidden under my coat. I still hadn't shown my neighbours my new weapons, as I wanted to get them all together in the morning to discuss Jerry joining us and then show them what he could bring to the party.

CHAPTER ELEVEN

Pete came round in the morning to report that a house in the next road had been burgled the previous night. When the man had fought back, they had shot and killed him and his entire family.

"We need to get everybody together right now," I told him. "We need to take more steps to protect ourselves. They're not just content with robbery now. They know there are no police and they're getting braver. They'll take any action, including murder, to take what we have."

Pete immediately went and rounded up the neighbours, including Allan, who we called on the walkie-talkie. He handed the meeting over to me, claiming that I was the expert on what we were about to discuss.

Expert! I thought. *All I've done is read a few books on the subject, but I suppose I have been preparing for this for a few years and so I do know a lot more about what to expect than most people here.*

I climbed on to the bonnet of a car and began my hastily prepared speech. "Friends, you've all heard what happened in the next road last night. Allan reckons the reason we've escaped the violence so far, is because we've been working together.

Those out there, who have resorted to violence and stealing, know that, and have had much easier targets to steal from. We're in a good position here at the moment, thanks to Allan sharing the supplies from the police station with us." There was a general murmuring and a quick round of applause directed at Allan, who blushed and held up his hands in recognition.

"With what Allan has, I reckon we have at least a couple months' worth of food available. If we're careful with it we won't need to worry about that for the moment. What we need to talk about is protecting what we have. Just walking about as we are at the moment won't deter them for much longer. Food is going to be getting scarcer by the day and soon whoever is out there will see us as the only place to get some."

"And why is that?" asked someone from the back.

"Because we're still here, being visible and obviously protecting something. If you didn't have food you'd have left in search of food elsewhere, like a lot of people have. But how much food is out there? The countryside must be swarming with people looking for food and there'll be some vegetables growing in fields, and animals as well. But how long are they going to last? I don't know the exact answer to that but I don't think it'll be long.

Winter's coming. Do you want to be sleeping in a tent or shelter when winter gets here? I certainly don't." I hadn't meant to go on so much, but I was getting into my stride and my prepper side was starting to show through. "Pete called you here because we need to start getting more serious about security. I'll set out what I think we need to do to try to stay safe. Then I'll hand you back over to Pete, so he can start getting it organised and, can I add, if you don't think this is necessary, then you need to question why you're still here!"

Probably a bit over the top as a speech, but then again, if they didn't want to take steps to protect our group more (including my family) then I personally didn't want them to stay. Over the years, I had given some thought to how I would protect my home, so now I just expanded my ideas to cover quite a few houses.

"At the moment we're spread out over too many houses. I suggest that the families living at the ends of the road either move into some of the empty houses near the middle or move in with friends. That way it'll be easier to help protect each other." That prompted a few moans and shakes of the head, but I continued.

"We'll block both ends of the road by creating a barrier of cars. This'll stop anybody coming down our road by accident. We'll then create another barrier where our houses are as our main line of defence; this'll have to be manned at all times. Our back gardens are vulnerable and could provide another way for us to be attacked.

I'll try to find enough barbed or razor wire to make a complete circle around all our properties. We can add to it and improve it as time goes on, but initially it should be sufficient to help protect us.

"As a few of you know, I own a few shotguns and Bob over there owns one as well. I'm willing to allow other people to use mine if they want to, to increase our fire power if need be. We also need to start collecting other things we can use as weapons, such as knives, cricket bats and golf clubs, and work out which will be best to use." I saw a few people start and look worried at the mention of guns and weapons, so I added, "Those of you who aren't looking too happy about the guns, think about that poor family on the next street last night and what he would have given for the chance of defending himself and his family and not letting some coward shoot him. Talking about weapons, do you remember me telling you on the first night about what had happened and what I'd learned from a bloke called Jerry via his brother in the army?"

Most people nodded. "Jerry lives not too far away in Kings Heath and I've been in regular contact with him by walkie-talkie. Yesterday I went to see him because his brother had sent him a crate with some things in and he wanted me to help him learn how to use them." I pulled the Glock out of the holster and the MP5 from where it had been slung on my back underneath my coat. "A few of these were in the crate and he's given me these to help protect us all. Jerry and his family are feeling vulnerable where they are, because nobody is helping anyone else in the way that we are here. His house was attacked yesterday, but he managed to scare them away. He's also a doctor and because he had advanced warning, he's very well stocked with medical supplies. I've invited him to come and live with us, and don't worry, he also has his own food supplies so he won't need to use any of ours. In fact, as I've got to know the man, I imagine he'll want to share some of them with us. I realise I don't need to ask your permission for someone to come and stay with me, but I would prefer it if you all agreed with my decision." I looked up and could see most people nodding in agreement. I wasn't sure if it was about my defence proposals or Jerry.

"How much food have you got then, Tom? You knew this was coming, you must have loads stashed away," shouted Rick from the crowd. My heart sank. I'd never got on with Rick.

I found him arrogant and called him "Rick the Prick" behind his back. He was one of the neighbours who had initially refused to help and only joined in when he saw the food Allan was giving us. He was constantly moaning about everything, from having to patrol in the middle of the night to how bland the food was.

He was starting to annoy most of the remaining street with his constant griping. Pete stared at him and said,

"Who cares what he's got? If you weren't so busy moaning all the time you'd have noticed that he's not taking any of the supplies Allan's giving us. He's using his own, which means there's been more for you, and if it wasn't for Tom, none of this would be happening. We'd all be starving by now and fighting each other for whatever we had left." He looked at everybody and carried on, "Does anyone else want to add anything?" Nobody spoke and most shot angry looks at Rick, which pleased me no end.

Pete stood up next to me on the car bonnet and I nodded my thanks to him. He asked if there were any questions about the defences or Jerry. Most seemed to accept my ideas as sensible, which I hoped they were. A few looked very uncomfortable about the idea of basically turning us into an armed camp, under siege in our own city. The idea seemed so foreign to most English people that some of them couldn't take it in, or accept it as being the only possible course of action.

Pete asked about Jerry and requested a show of hands from anyone happy for him to join us.

I was relieved when they all put their hands up. At least they could see the benefit of having a fully equipped doctor among us.

Pete quickly showed his leadership skills, organising work parties to start moving cars in order to form the initial barricade, and starting a list of the residents who would benefit by moving, so that he could find out if they would.

I got on the walkie-talkie and called Jerry to give him the good news. He was ecstatic, as last night the gang had returned and had tried to break in through his front door. He had ended up firing the Glock, in sheer terror, through the door at them. He sounded as if he was in shock and apologised for not checking on the Land Rover, as he hadn't wanted to leave the house because that would mean leaving his family. I told Becky what had happened to Jerry, and she immediately agreed that they must come and stay with us and that I should go over and help him straight away. I called him back.

"Jerry, I'm on my way over to help, but start getting some supplies out of the cellar and stacked in the hallway. I'll explain my plan to you when I arrive."

CHAPTER TWELVE

I found Pete and told him where I was going and that Jerry had a theory about getting a car started, so not to be surprised if we turned up in one. For speed, I put a car battery and a few tools into a rucksack and got my mountain bike from the garage. Car batteries are heavy things, so I was a bit uncomfortable as I pedalled up the road with the rucksack on my back and the MP5 slung around my front. When I was just past the High Street there was a shout from behind me. Looking back, I saw a couple of youths starting to chase after me. That made me forget how heavy the rucksack was and I turned into Chris Hoy. It's amazing how fast you can cycle when you need to. I soon lost them, and a few minutes later I arrived at Jerry's house.

Jerry opened the door and helped me to get the bike into the house.

"Let's not waste any time," I said. "I need you to keep sorting what supplies you want to take first, and that definitely includes the guns. I'll help you, because if I manage to get the Land Rover started, we're really going to have to get a move on." What I was planning to do, as soon as I got the car started and drove it round to Jerry's house, was to get Fiona and the two kids in and fill the back of the car, and whatever space was left, with the first load of supplies.

Then I'd quickly drop them off at my street, hook up my trailer and head back to get Jerry and another load of stuff, hopefully without attracting too much attention.

I called Becky on the walkie-talkie.

"Becky, can you get the trailer ready, and get hold of Pete for me?" I quickly filled him in on the plan and asked him to make sure we had enough people available to help unload the supplies. I didn't want to leave Jerry on his own for too long, so a quick turnaround would be essential.

For the next hour Jerry, Fiona and I carried supplies up from the cellar and stacked them by the front door in the order in which we wanted to load them. We weren't sure how much we were going to be able to take with us, but eventually the pile looked big enough and I called a halt. The first things to be loaded would be the ammunition, baby and medical supplies and clothes. Then we would need as much food as we could cram in. We pulled the shelf unit back over the door to conceal it. It hid the doorway completely.

We were ready to go. Jerry told me where the car was. It was just around the corner so I decided to walk. The Land Rover was parked on the drive of an obviously empty house (the door had been kicked in, and items from inside were strewn across the drive).

At least I won't have an angry owner to face while I'm attempting to steal his pride and joy, I thought, as I looked the car over.

It was one I recognised, because I'd seen it driving around the area. Its owner and I had always waved at each other as we passed, congratulating ourselves on our taste in transport. It was a long-wheelbase model about the same age as mine, but it had a large cage-type metal roof rack on top with sides about six inches tall on them. I'd brought tools with me, so that I could take the ignition apart and hot-wire it, but thankfully the keys were in the ignition, probably left there in disgust when it didn't start, and then forgotten about.

I lifted the passenger seat, underneath which the battery sits, and quickly changed the batteries over, tightened up the connections and closed the bonnet. Looking round, I could see a man looking at me through the window of a house opposite. He didn't look threatening so I ignored him. I radioed Jerry.

"Right, Jerry, I'm going to try to start the car."

"Okay. Good luck," came the reply from him, and also from Becky, who was listening in.

Turning the key, I held my breath. The engine turned over, but didn't catch. I tried again and this time it caught, but as I was feathering the throttle the engine died after a few beats.

"Come on!" I screamed at it, "Don't do this to me now, you can do it!" She must have been listening and been sorry for messing me about, because on the third attempt she caught and after a few seconds of bubbling along, settled down to a steady beat. "Thank you, my darling, I'm sorry I shouted at you," I muttered, as I put it in gear ready to drive off. The driver's door was suddenly pulled open and a hand reached in to grab me. It was the man from the house opposite. I instinctively swung out with my right arm and my elbow caught him in the face. He stumbled and fell backwards. I looked at him. He was about fifty, and quite a small bloke. I put the Land Rover back into neutral as he got up and started to come towards me again. I pulled the Glock out of the holster and pointed it at him. He stopped in his tracks and held his arms out.

"What the hell are you doing?" I screamed at him, "If you take one more step towards me, I'll shoot and believe me I don't want to do that!"

"Please, I'm sorry, we haven't eaten for days and we're starving" pleaded the man, breaking down in tears.

I looked beyond him and at the doorway of the house he'd come from, stood a woman I presumed was his wife, and three teenage kids.

My God, it had only been a few weeks and this man, who looked as mild mannered and timid as anyone I'd ever seen, was trying to attack me for what he thought I had. My anger changed instantly to compassion. The walkie-talkie bleeped and Jerry came on to find out if everything was OK. I quickly replied, telling him that I would be there in a minute and to get ready.

I thought for a second and lowered my gun. "Look, if you follow me round the corner and help me load this car for a friend of mine, we'll give you some food as a thank you."

He nodded and seemed relieved. I put the car into gear and drove quickly round to Jerry's house, acutely aware of the noise I was making. As I backed on to his drive, we immediately put Larry and Jack into the back of the car. I opened the rear door and started to pile the crate from his brother and the medical supplies, and boxes and boxes of food into it. As we were loading I explained to Jerry what had happened, and the offer I had made to the man. He agreed that it was the right decision to make. The man promptly turned up with two of his children. I thanked them for trusting me and immediately got them to start loading boxes into the roof rack. One of them climbed up and the other two passed them up. In less than ten minutes we had it all loaded and were ready to go.

"Right, now here's what's happening," I explained to the man, "Jerry's staying here and I'll be back in about ten minutes to load up again. Then we'll give you some food."

He nodded as Fiona and I jumped into the car and drove off. As I looked in my rear-view mirror, I could see Jerry leading the man and his boys into the house. I passed the walkie-talkie to Fiona and told her to say we were two minutes away and that they should get ready.

I couldn't drive too fast because I was having to steer around all the cars abandoned in the road. However, it only took a couple of minutes to get there. When we pulled into the road, I could see that the car barricade had been completed, but cleverly, a gap had been left in the middle so that I could drive the car through. Becky immediately took charge of Fiona and the kids and took them straight into our house. Pete, true to his word, had about ten of the neighbours waiting to help, so it only took a few minutes to unload all the goods. I then turned the Land Rover around, hooked up the trailer and got ready to drive off. Allan jumped into the passenger seat, saying he wanted to help. Who was I to refuse?

As we drove back, I said, "Only don't give me a ticket, because I haven't connected the electrics, so the trailer brake lights won't be working."

He kept a straight face, and replied, "I'm more concerned that the car isn't displaying a tax disc," and he ripped it off the windscreen and threw it out of the side window. "Anyway, I'm not up to date on the law, but the last time I checked, having a machine gun across your lap and a pistol on your hip meant at least a couple of points on your licence."

"Touché!" I replied, laughing.

Driving back to Jerry's house, a few people must have heard the car passing the first time and come out of their houses to see what was happening. Most of them looked haggard and thin and just stared in amazement, as the first working car they had seen in a few weeks drove past. Some shouted for us to stop, when they saw a man in a police uniform in the front seat. Others just held their arms out in a silent appeal for help.

The sight sobered us up immediately. "Allan," I said quietly, "we can't help them all, we just can't, and if we do, then in a few short weeks, we'll be just as desperate as those poor sods."

"I know," he replied solemnly, "I have thought about distributing more of the supplies, but I know it would just be a drop in the ocean, given what these people need, and soon we'd all have nothing left. I've already decided just to help your group, and was thinking about asking if I can come and join you."

"I'm sure you'd be more than welcome, but let's discuss it later. This is Jerry's house now."

Backing up on the drive, Jerry already had the door open and with his helpers, was bringing out boxes of supplies. I quickly introduced Allan and Jerry to each other and they shook hands. We then got on with loading the car and trailer, as we now had a lot more space in the car and it was going to take longer to get finished, which was worrying.

A few minutes later, I looked up and saw a group of men approaching us. I warned Allan and told him it would probably be better if he spoke to them, as the sight of his uniform might buy us some time. I grabbed my MP5 out of the car and told Jerry, who already had his slung over his shoulder, to go and get the shotgun out of the house. We carried on loading the supplies as quickly as we could. I could hear Allan using what I presumed to be his best policeman voice, telling the growing crowd to go back home and let us carry on with our business. I could tell they weren't having any of it. I said to myself, *Time to act a lot braver than you feel*, and grabbing Jerry's pump-action shotgun, I walked over to back Allan up. People took a step back as I approached. I must have looked very intimidating. I had a pistol in a holster, a machine gun on my back and was carrying a mean looking shotgun.

Calmly but clearly, I said, "Go home, there's nothing for you here. I'm here to help a friend move some of his things and I've asked PC Harris here to come along and make sure nothing happens to his private property. I don't want to hurt anybody, but if anybody threatens any of us, PC Harris has authorised me, in accordance with the emergency powers he's operating under, to use deadly force if necessary." I was making it up as I went along, but I thought it sounded plausible. It must have done, because the crowd, which had grown to about twenty people, seemed to take a few steps back. A voice from the back shouted,

"We've got no food. You can't stop us taking it." I saw a few men push to the front carrying crow bars and golf clubs. Beside me, Allan whispered,

"Don't take a step back. As soon as we do, they'll be on us." I glanced behind me and saw Jerry and the man with his two sons, feverishly loading up the Land Rover and trailer. I raised the shotgun to my shoulder and pumped a cartridge into the chamber.

A few of the crowd decided they'd seen enough, pushed their way to the back and left.

Come on, Jerry. Bloody hurry up! I screamed silently to myself.

"You can't stop us, we're not in a police state," shouted the unknown voice from the back again.

At that moment, I would have gladly shot the coward who was standing at the back, trying to get the crowd to do his dirty work for him. But he wasn't going to show himself. A few more tense minutes passed.

Suddenly a rock was thrown, which bounced off the side of the Land Rover. *"That's it!"* I decided. *"No more pratting about!"* I stepped forward, pointed the shotgun over the heads of the crowd and fired a shot. I pumped the action again to load another cartridge, pointed it at the men in the front row and shouted "That's the last warning shot I'm going to fire. The next person who takes a step forward, I'll shoot, and at this range it'll cut you in half!" That did it. The crowd turned and ran, shouting obscenities as they fled.

Allan looked at me and said, "Rambo look out! And what the hell are those emergency powers?" I handed the shotgun to him and said,

"Hold this for a moment will you, I think I'm going to be sick and I'm about to wet myself." I promptly ran over to the front garden wall and threw up over it. So much for Rambo!

The Land Rover and trailer were now fully loaded. I don't think they could have squeezed one more tin of beans into it, or on to the roof rack. We thanked our helpers, and after getting Jerry's permission, told them they could have all the supplies that were left in the hallway of the house.

I asked them if they were going to be all right getting them home. They had worked out that their gardens almost backed on to each other and as the houses in between were empty now, they could make a few trips by passing the boxes over the fences.

He apologised again for attacking me and thanked us all profusely for the food. We wished them luck and headed home, opting for an alternative route to avoid passing the people we had seen earlier. Allan got on the radio.

"We're on our way back. Expect us in five minutes."

CHAPTER THIRTEEN

As soon as we were back in the road, Pete gave orders for the gap in the barricade to be closed by pushing the waiting car in front of it. Plenty of people appeared to help unload the supplies from the Land Rover and trailer. On the drive back I talked to Jerry about his supplies.

"I think it would be a great idea if you offered some of your supplies to the community as a thank you gift. You needn't worry because, with what you've got left hidden back at your house, together with what I've got in storage, we'll have enough to feed both our families for a very long time. Giving some away would be a good way of deflecting any jealousy when people see what we're unloading."

While Jerry introduced himself to everyone who had gathered round to help, I organised a chain of people to help carry the supplies into the house.

There was an appreciative round of applause when I told them all that Jerry was going to donate a part of what he had to the road. The remaining supplies still made an impressive pile once they were all unloaded and stacked in our hallway.

We showed Jerry and Fiona the spare bedroom in which Becky had thoughtfully set up a travel cot for Jack, and a blow-up bed for Larry. Becky and Fiona had hit it off immediately.

Becky couldn't stop fussing over Jack as her maternal instincts kicked in the way that they do, when any woman with older children comes within ten feet of a young baby. I just knew that in bed later, Becky would start talking about how nice it would be for Stanley and Daisy to have a little brother or sister.

Well, at least this time I'll have a great excuse. After all, the end of the world as we know it, is happening outside our bedroom window! Surely she'll see sense?

I showed Jerry the supplies I had stored in the garage and the playroom.

He was very impressed with how much we had, and how we'd organised it so that any items we needed could easily be reached.

Pete and Allan dropped in to see how Jerry and his family were settling in. Pete gave me an update on how the road's defence plan was going. Both ends of the road now had a barrier of cars across and most of the neighbours who lived at the ends of the road had seen the sense in moving closer together. The arrangements to move into either one of the empty houses, or in with friends, were progressing nicely. A lot more work needed to be done, but it was a start, and at least the neighbours were mostly all cooperating.

Allan arranged to move in with Pete and his family. He was going to spend tonight and probably most of tomorrow at the police station, sorting out what equipment they had stored there, and getting it ready to be moved. We discussed using the car and trailer, but when Allan and I told Pete what had happened at Jerry's house we all agreed that it was best not to attract any more attention than we already had.

The patrols and the barricading of the road were bound to be noticed and make any outsiders wonder what we were protecting. If they knew we had a working car, it would probably make them even more determined to try to take it from us, along with anything else we had.

As we sat around my kitchen table, a shout and the sound of the Land Rover starting made us all run to the front door. We saw the car speeding up the road and swerving around the neighbours as they tried to stop it. As it slowed down to get through the barricade, I saw that the car that had been blocking the entrance had already been rolled out of the way. At this point a man called Ian stood in front of the Land Rover to stop it, but instead it ploughed into him with a sickening thud, knocked him partially out of the way, then ran over his legs as it sped away. It turned on to the High Street and disappeared from view.

Pete, Jerry, Allan and I ran up to the barricade, shouting at the people who were out on the street, trying to find out what had happened.

"It was Rick and the Coles!" one of them shouted back. "They were on patrol at the barricade. I saw them push the car out of the way, then they ran to the car, got all their families inside it and drove off. It happened so quickly we couldn't stop them."

Jerry was kneeling on the floor next to Ian, who looked in a bad way. "Go and get my Trauma Kit; it's in the hall of your house. You can't miss it, it's a green rucksack with a white cross on it!" he shouted at me. I ran back to my house, grabbed the bag and brought it back to Jerry.

"He's dead," Pete said softly as I returned, "Jerry thinks his neck is broken."

Mary, Ian's wife, ran up and knelt next to him, screaming for Jerry to do something. Jerry put a hand on her shoulder, said something quietly to her, stood up and walked over to us.

"I'm sorry. There was nothing I could do. I think he died as soon as he hit the road. He landed badly and broke his neck." He was quiet for a moment and then said, "Who did it? Did we know them?"

"Yes!" I replied angrily, "But let's try and help Mary. I'll tell you later."

More of the wives had arrived. The men all took a step back and stood there watching the tragedy, as emotions spilled over and the women tried to comfort Mary. Everybody had a tear in their eye and a big lump in their throat. Ian had been a lovely man. He'd been retired, and had always had time to chat to everybody on the road, and was a regular at the social occasions the Residents Committee organised throughout the year. They'd celebrated their fiftieth wedding anniversary earlier in the year by holding a big party in a marquee in their back garden and most of us had been invited.

The children had started to gather round as well. I indicated to a few people standing close by to take them away.

It wasn't right that they should have to witness the grief and agony that was unfolding out in the road. A thoughtful neighbour arrived with a sheet and Jerry draped it over Ian's body.

A group of us walked past the barricade to the junction of our road and the High Street. We stood around, waiting to be needed by our wives, who were trying to comfort an obviously inconsolable Mary. A noise caught our attention. Looking up, we saw a large group of about thirty men approaching.

CHAPTER FOURTEEN

Most were carrying weapons of some sort, but about five were carrying shotguns. We all turned and ran back to the barricade and I screamed at the women, "Move it NOW! There's a group of thugs approaching. They must have heard the Land Rover leaving. You must leave now. Gather all the children, go to my house and lock the door."

I watched the now distraught women run down the road, dragging or carrying the children with them, towards my house. I suddenly realised that apart from the handguns Jerry and I were carrying, nobody else had any weapons on them. We'd all just reacted and run to the barricade when Rick had driven through it, leaving the MP5s and shotguns leaning up against the wall in the kitchen. I ran back to my house hoping that the door wasn't already locked. It wasn't and Becky, having seen our guns in the kitchen, was already carrying them through the house.

I threw my gun safe keys at her and told her to go and unlock it and bring them all up along with some more ammunition. I ran back to the barricade loaded down with the guns. I gave Jerry his MP5 and handed the pump-action shotgun to Allan. Looking round, I noticed that most of the other men now had a weapon of some sort in their hands.

The car had been pushed back to complete the barricade and I was glad that at least someone was thinking. The gang had now arrived at the top of the road and were looking at us crouched behind the line of cars. There were only about fifteen of us.

"Where is everybody else?" I asked.

"A few will be at the other barricade, but I don't know where the others are," Pete replied. Becky and another neighbour arrived, carrying five shotguns and a bag of cartridges. I asked who knew how to use them and keeping one, passed them over to the ones who had said they could, telling them to grab a handful of cartridges from the bag, but to keep out of sight and not to show the guns yet.

One of the gang walked towards the barricade, carrying a shotgun over his shoulder. Pete stood up unarmed and shouted, "Stop right there, we've got nothing for you and if you attack, we'll defend ourselves."

"Defend yourselves with what?" he sneered. "You're just a bunch of old men, you can't stop us! I'm going to give you one minute to move away and show us what food you have and you won't get hurt. Or we'll just come over and take it from you. If we have to do that, we're going to hurt you all badly." He turned and walked back up to his men.

It was like a scene from a movie with a bad script, but it was happening right on our road. Crouching behind the car, I spoke to all the men holding guns. "Look, those people are going to attack and if they get through us, who knows what they'll do to our families? I've already been attacked once today over at Jerry's and words aren't going to stop them. Only these," I held up my shotgun. "You have to be prepared to use them to protect yourself and your family…"

I was stopped by the leader shouting, "Time's up!" The gang started to walk towards us. Pete again bravely stood up, shouting, "We have guns! Don't come any closer!" This caused a few of them to falter, but the leader raised his shotgun and shouted, "So do we!" and fired both barrels at Pete, who just managed to duck behind the car.

"NOW!" I yelled. We all stood up and those of us with guns pointed them at the now running mob. Another one fired his gun at us, but because he was running, the shot went high. At the sound of the shot we all instinctively pulled our triggers. Our first shots ripped into the rapidly approaching mob. I had a second to notice that even at that range a few shots must have missed, because a lot of them still seemed to be coming at us.

I fired my second barrel and realising I wouldn't have time to reload, reached for the MP5 slung across my back. Allan was blazing away with the pump-action and Jerry was shooting his gun in three-shot bursts. All the others were frantically trying to reload the unfamiliar shotguns and firing wildly at the attackers, or were swinging whatever weapon they had at the men who were beginning to climb over the barricade. I fired at the man nearest to me and watched him fall. I shot again and again until my gun clicked empty. I reloaded as quickly as my shaking hands would let me.

Looking back on it now, at that moment, when we were being attacked for the first time and were using deadly force to protect ourselves and our loved ones, we were aware that people were being killed, but in the terror of the situation, we knew it was either them or us, and we did what we had to do. We would all look back with a sick feeling about what we'd had to do, and most of us would have nightmares or sleepless nights reliving the moment.

But at the time it felt right; the only course of action to take. We had to survive and if someone was trying to kill us, the natural thing to do was to kill them first, if we could.

They couldn't take the punishment we were giving them, and after about thirty seconds (although it seemed like a lifetime), the survivors turned and ran. One of them swung round and aimed his shotgun at us, and both Jerry and I raised our guns and fired. He was flung backwards as six bullets hit him.

Silence settled over the road as the gunfire ceased. As the ringing in our ears slowly subsided, we could hear the screams and groans of wounded men. Looking around, we all seemed to be OK. There were a few cuts and bruises and Pete was holding his arm awkwardly after being hit by a rock. But we were all alive. The bodies of our attackers were on the cars of the barricade and on the road before it, most with horrific gunshot wounds. Shotguns at close range are devastating.

We stood there in a daze, trying to take in what we had done and the fact that we had survived. Jerry, standing beside me with tears streaming down his face, looked at the dead and dying, and said softly, "I'm a bloody doctor, I'm meant to save people not kill them."

"Look mate, we had to do it. Do you think they would have been happy just taking our food? No, they had guns and fired first. They'd probably have killed us all, and taken our wives and children as sex slaves while they continued terrorising whoever is left around here. We've done the area a favour by getting rid of them.

That's the way I'm going to look at it and you should too. We all should. It's the only way we'll cope with what we've just had to do." I felt myself changing as I said the words. I'd just killed people who were trying to kill me and my friends. I'd probably have to do it again and, strangely, it didn't feel wrong.

Allan walked over to us, blood from a wound running down his face.

He was very calm, possibly because of his training, or perhaps because it hadn't been his family or his home he had just saved. He snapped us out of it by taking control and issuing orders. "Doc, check our people and make sure no one's badly wounded. Look at Pete first. His arm looks pretty bad."

"But what about them?" replied Jerry, waving his arm at the wounded in front of the barricade.

"NO! Our people first, then see if you can help any of those scum," came the blunt reply. He was trying to separate our emotions. They were the enemy. Just a few minutes before, they had been shooting at us and trying to kill us. We needed to look after ourselves first.

Allan sent Bob back down the road to tell the families sheltering in our house that we were all OK, but they were to stay inside until we told them it was safe to come out.

Standing by the barricade, he looked at the dead and wounded and turned back to us, looking horrified. "Ian's under that lot, we didn't move him!" That galvanised us into action. We pulled a few dead bodies out of the way until we reached Ian's body. Four of us passed him gently over the barricade and laid him on the pavement next to Pete, who was sitting against the wall with his arm in a makeshift splint. He was white faced and clearly in shock. After a quick assessment, Jerry confirmed that his arm was broken.

We began checking the attackers. We moved the dead to one side and the injured to the other, where Jerry got to work on helping them. In total, there were fifteen dead and ten wounded, some seriously and some with a few shotgun pellets in their arms or legs. Those that appeared to have the least life-threatening injuries seemed to be moaning the loudest, swearing and shouting for us to help them.

Jerry stood up from checking the most seriously injured and said he didn't think he could save most of them. They needed surgery and he just didn't have the expertise or equipment to do it. "What are we going to do with them?" asked one of the neighbours. This started a heated discussion, with some people saying we should let them die and others saying that if we didn't try to help them, we risked losing our humanity and would be just as bad as them.

I didn't know which side I agreed with, as I could see both points of view and couldn't decide until Jerry spoke up saying:

"Stop it! Shut up everybody! Look, I'm the only one here with medical experience and I'll do my best to save them but if, in my opinion, I can't and they're too far gone to help, and extending their life will only increase their suffering, then God forgive me, I'll give them an overdose of morphine. It's all I can think to do."

That stopped the discussion immediately. I think we were all glad that the decision had been taken out of our hands, and we left Jerry to treat them. We had to restrain the less severely injured, as Jerry injected local anaesthetic and removed lead shot gun pellets from arms, legs and bodies. Once they were treated, Allan plasti-cuffed their arms and legs to stop them trying to escape and to prevent them from attacking us. Looking at the demoralised survivors, I think the fight had gone out of them.

Becky arrived. I thought about telling her off, but as she was carrying a shotgun I decided not to. "Is everyone OK?" she asked anxiously.

"Yes, my love, we're all fine. Pete's broken his arm and there are a few cuts and bruises. What are you doing here anyway? We sent Bob to tell you it's over and we're OK." I took her to one side and continued.

"The point is, my love, there are quite a few dead bodies we need to move and we haven't decided what to do with the injured yet. I need you to keep everyone in our house until I come and get you. We'll try and sort this bloody mess out."

"But what happened? How did this happen?" she asked, looking around at our shocked looking faces and the dead and the wounded lying on and beyond our barricade.

"We had no choice. They must have been attracted by that idiot Rick, stealing the Land Rover. They probably knew we were here, but when they saw the car leaving, they decided to see what else we were hiding. They had guns and fired first, so we had to defend ourselves. If you hadn't been fantastic and brought up my extra guns, I don't know if we'd have been able to stop them. I can't believe that bloody fool killed Ian in his desperation to get away. And the Coles going with him! They were meant to be our friends!"

Becky looked at me, took my hands in hers and said, "You've done the right thing, you've kept us alive and those people were going to take it all away from us. I'll go back and try to calm everybody down. We need to let Mary grieve after what that bastard did to Ian. I'll try to keep everybody busy." As she turned to walk away another thought came to me, so I called her back.

Quietly, I said, "A few of the men seem to have gone missing. Can you do a headcount when you get back and try and work out who they are? I'll do the same here and we'll talk later."

"Why?" she asked.

"Because the rest of us risked our lives to protect their families, and if people think they can hide at the first sign of trouble, then the way I'm feeling at the moment, they can bloody well leave." Becky nodded and turned to walk back home.

Allan was still doing an excellent job. He had sent a few men to relieve the ones at the other barricade and had others picking up the guns and other weapons dropped by our attackers.

He knew that keeping us all busy was the best way, in the short term, to help us deal with what we had just experienced. He came over to me and asked if I would give him a hand questioning the survivors.

"Of course," I said, "but why me?"

"Well," he replied, "if I don't seem to be getting anywhere, I'm sure if you pull that big pistol of yours out and look a bit crazy, it'll help loosen their tongues. A bit more bad cop, worse cop than good cop, bad cop. We need to find out about this gang and if there are any more of them."

As it turned out I didn't need to intimidate them, as Allan did a great job of extracting all the information. It was good to see some old-fashioned policing, with the odd slap round the head and a threat of something more painful to get most of them talking. Cowards, the lot of them. As a group, they'd felt big and strong, but separated from their comrades and questioned individually, they soon broke down and were begging Allan to stop so that they could tell him everything.

CHAPTER FIFTEEN

They appeared to be the main gang that had been terrorising the neighbourhood, stealing from shops and houses as soon as the EMP hit. The gang had grown in strength as more like-minded people had joined them, and as the food became scarcer, they started breaking into people's houses to find provisions. As each robbery went by, they became more confident and dangerous. Realising that they could get away with any crime they committed, it hadn't taken them long to start killing anyone who put up any resistance, and soon after that, killing just for fun.

The previous week, as their numbers had increased, they had taken over a large house on St Agnes Road, killing the starving family who were living there. They had been systematically breaking into every house on most of the roads in the neighbourhood, killing the occupants and taking whatever supplies they had.

Sometimes they kept the prettier women and girls as playthings, replacing them as soon as fresher ones were found. The shotguns had been picked up at various houses they had raided.

They knew about us and had avoided us, because there were easier pickings to be had.

When they'd seen the car driving away, as I'd suggested to Becky earlier, we'd become too tempting a target not to attack.

There were still a few of them left at the house, guarding the women they were keeping as sex slaves. The group that had attacked us made up the rest of them. We need to rescue those women, was my first thought. I proposed a rescue mission to Allan.

"No!" he said immediately, "We're in a mess here and the ones who ran off will have got back to their base by now. Are any of us up for another fight at the moment? Yes, I agree we should help them, but we need to look after ourselves first and then get a plan together."

He was speaking sense, and we definitely had a lot of work to do before we could let our children back out on the street. We discussed what we would do with the dead and the prisoners. Allan suggested that we take the ones who could walk up to the police station, where we could lock them in the cells until we decided what to do with them. It was a sensible idea, so a few neighbours acted as sentries, following Allan and the hobbling, pathetic murderers up to the police station. I helped Pete to walk back down to my house so that the women could look after him. Jerry had told him to rest and take some of the painkillers he had given him.

At home Becky had things well organised. The children were watching a DVD in one room while some of the women fussed round Mary, who was sitting quietly in a corner still obviously very distressed. The others were making food for the hungry DVD viewers.

Jack, Jerry and Fiona's baby was being spoilt rotten with all the fuss and attention he was getting. I gave her a quick résumé of what was happening and what we had found out about the gang, including our desire to rescue the women who were being kept prisoner. She agreed that we needed to rescue them, but didn't want any of us to put ourselves at risk by doing so.

I helped her to make a couple of trays of tea and we carried them out to the rest of the men, who were still working to clear the mess around the barricade. We'd gathered six shotguns, about two hundred cartridges and also a variety of weapons, including a very sharp looking Samurai sword, from the dead and wounded. Looking at the weapons, I couldn't help but think they would make a valuable contribution to our defence capabilities.

Jerry came over to me, saying that all but one of the seriously wounded had died and he didn't expect the last one to live much longer. I didn't ask him if they had died naturally or if he had helped them.

It was his decision to make and I didn't want to question it. I trusted him to do the right thing.

We had twenty-one bodies to dispose of. We would have to move them away from our street, but where to? And should we bury them or cremate them? This was a difficult decision because neither solution was straightforward. Burying that many people would take a very large hole and, to be honest, none of us wanted to spend a lot of time and effort digging a grave for people who had been trying to kill us. But we were still trying to hold on to our sense of morality and decency. If not, we would turn into people like our attackers.

In the end it was agreed by a majority vote, that we would use my trailer to take the bodies in a few trips up to a building site a few roads away. There we would build a funeral pyre and burn the bodies. We used whatever pallets and wood we could find on the site and a good soaking of petrol.

Jim, one of the neighbours, volunteered to say a few words before we lit the pyre. It was the only thing we could do. We were sure that before long we would be faced with the same dilemma again. But we couldn't have bodies rotting in the street, spreading diseases and being eaten by the increasing number of animals and rodents roaming around.

As it was getting late, with only a few hours of daylight left, we had to get a move on, as we didn't want to leave the bodies until the morning.

Leaving a few people behind to man the barricades, we took three trips to move the bodies, while a few of the others built up a large stack of timber to form the pyre.

I used a hammer and screwdriver to knock a hole in the petrol tank of a nearby car and collected a few buckets of petrol. Then we liberally doused the pyre with it. As we gathered around in the growing dusk, Jim spoke up with his hastily prepared speech.

"God, please take these poor souls into your care. In their desperation to survive, they lost their way and we are truly sorry we had to speed their passing. I hope you can forgive them as we have done, as they have now paid the ultimate price for their temporary loss of humanity. Amen."

I lit a rag, tied it round a length of timber, and making sure we were all clear of the pyre, threw it on top of it. The petrol ignited with a loud whoosh and we all stood for a few minutes watching the pyre burning, each lost in our own thoughts. "Come on," said Allan. "We should be getting back now, it's getting dark and I'm sure your wives will be missing you." We were a silent group as we walked back to our road, tired to the bone after the day we'd experienced.

CHAPTER SIXTEEN

When we got back, the men gathered their wives and children and started to drift back to their own homes. Bob and his wife Jo, not wanting Mary to go back to her empty house, took her home with them. Pete, now that Jerry had set his arm in a proper cast, was looking much more comfortable, and had spent his time while we were outside, clearing up and re-working the rotas, now that Rick and the Coles had run away. I raised the issue about the neighbours who had disappeared at the first sign of trouble on the barricade.

"I know, Tom. Becky and I sat down and we've worked out who we think they are." He showed me the list and I agreed with it. There were five names on it, and thinking about them as individuals, you could describe them as the more academic members of our community.

"What do you propose we do?" I asked.

"I'll find them in the morning, speak to them all separately and listen to what excuses they have to give. Look Tom, I know this situation we're in is something you've obviously been thinking about for quite a while now, and so you're far more mentally, materially and physically prepared than the rest of us. I'll probably give them all the benefit of the doubt this time. But if it happens again, then there'll be no more excuses.

The rest of us stood up to be counted when it mattered and as a collective, we'll all have to work together to protect and cherish what we have, for as long as we can. If some of them aren't prepared to do that, then their presence here will have to be questioned."

It was quite a speech and Pete had obviously given it a lot of thought. In my view, he'd got it exactly right. We did have to work together, but I was going to have to think very carefully about the way things were at the moment.

All the preparations I'd made over the past few years, especially in the days preceding the event, had been about feeding and protecting my immediate and, if necessary, extended family. We had started the food bank on an impulse, when we realised we had collected more than enough supplies and would still have the opportunity to collect more. So we'd begun to allocate half of everything we'd collected, to be given to friends and neighbours when the need arose. But there were about twenty families still on the road, at least eighty people. It was going to take a tremendous amount to feed them all.

Even with my food bank and Allan's supplies from the police station, it was only going to last for so long. With winter approaching, the food that nature could provide us with, from vegetable gardens and from foraging for wild edible plants, would be significantly reduced.

I had to think about whether we wanted to be part of the collective or whether it was best for us to be on our own.

The first meal we shared with Jerry and Fiona, after the children had showered and settled down to sleep, was a very quiet affair. We were all completely drained after the events of the day. I wasn't on sentry duty, so after the meal I opened a bottle of Becky's homemade damson gin. We settled down on the sofas in front of the log burner for a night cap. The alcohol relaxed us all and the conversation flowed around our anxieties about our families and friends around the country and how they were coping.

Jerry and Fiona were very happy to have joined us, admitting that it was the first time in weeks they'd felt able to relax, knowing that others were out there right now protecting us. They couldn't stop thanking us.

Jerry had said that Fiona had given up her job when the children arrived, but I'd never got around to asking what she did.

"Well, I was a dentist and decided to take a career break to raise the children. I always intended to return to it once both children were at school."

"Jerry and Fiona, it's a pleasure to have you with us. If you decide to stay with us, or move into one of the empty houses, that's up to you. The fact that you're a doctor and have brought supplies with you is great and everybody has already, as you know, voted to allow you to join us. As soon as they find out Fiona is a dentist, they'll all be over the moon!"

Jerry knew about my car and asked me about it.

"Mm. The incident with the Land Rover only happened today, people haven't yet made the connection that mine will probably be working as well. As a precaution, I've been in the garage, taken out the battery and disabled the car by removing and hiding the spark plugs and solenoid. I don't want to run the risk of my car, and someone wanting it, becoming another potential flashpoint. If people ask, I'll say, yes, it does work, but it's been disabled to avoid temptation and it will only be used if everyone is in agreement. I hope they'll all have enough trust in me."

We discussed the supplies that were still hidden at their house. Jerry said,

"I think we should treat them as our emergency stash and avoid telling anyone about them. What do you think?"

"I agree, and it would probably be a good idea at some point to go back to the house and fix the shelf unit against the wall in to hide the doorway properly, just in case someone searches your cellar and accidentally uncovers it."

The talk led to the morality of what we had done today. I told them how, only this morning, I'd been physically sick with fear after confronting the gang at Jerry's house, but just a short time later, I'd had no hesitation in shooting at and most probably killing, quite a few people. Jerry summed it up by saying,

"I'm a doctor, and as such, I've sworn to offer my help to all in need, but things are different now. They have to be. I didn't want to shoot and kill those people today, or do what I had to do to the seriously injured afterwards.

But if I hadn't, we wouldn't be sitting here now and people would be suffering needlessly. We're going to have to be strong to survive in the future, otherwise we'll just fade away, or someone will come and take it from us. We may be judged at some point, but I hope it will be seen that we did our best to keep our decency and humanity."

"Well said, Jerry!" Becky replied. "If it hadn't been for all your bravery today, the possibilities of what could have happened don't bear thinking about. I've no doubt that you'll all do your best to protect us all. We can't judge you if the only course of action is to kill someone if they're trying to kill you, or anyone else in our group. As you rightly said, Jerry, things are different now, and until some order or government is formed again in the future, we have the right to do what we need to do to survive, according to our own moral compass." Tears started to roll down her cheeks, so I pulled her into a hug and told her I loved her.

"I think we've all had enough for today. Let's go to bed and hope that tomorrow is a bit calmer," I said quietly. Nobody disagreed, so we bade each other goodnight. I talked to Becky about whether it was best for our family to stay and work together with our neighbours, or to go it alone. We discussed the merits of trying to get to our house in Wales, or using the caravan. In the end we both decided that we would feel safer if we stayed at our house. As long as all the neighbours were working together, it would be a lot better than being on our own.

It rained heavily that night which was a blessing, as it washed the street clear of all the blood.

CHAPTER SEVENTEEN

Pete called a meeting of all the neighbours early in the morning, saying that he had a few items he wanted to discuss with us all.

"Obviously, yesterday's terrible events have brought up questions of security. I have measures I think we need to implement. I want to put Allan in charge of road security. He will be responsible for making sure our defences are sufficient, and will also recommend any improvements or changes that need to be made." Pete was a very organised man and had drawn up a "job description", which he wanted us all to approve.

"Allan will be responsible for training everyone, so that in the event of an emergency, we will all know immediately where to go and what to do. If he needs help, he'll arrange it through me, so that the best person or people can be allocated to him."

A few people queried Pete's right to tell any of us what to do, which in normal circumstances, would be a fair and reasonable question and was one, I think, which Pete was expecting. He gave a stirring speech.

"This is the reality. If we all work together, as we are doing at the moment, we will survive. And yes, nobody has the right to order any of us around, but hopefully my requests will be reasonable and I will do my best to divide the hard or menial tasks fairly among us.

If anyone thinks they are being unfairly treated then all they have to do is speak to me."

After giving the matter some thought, most people could see the sense in it, so most indicated their agreement. The next item on his agenda was food and cooking.

"As far as cooking goes, we need to make better use of the supplies we have by cooking it collectively. At the moment, if people need food, they help themselves from the boxes that Allan has given us.

This has obviously led to wastage, both in the fuel that's being used for cooking and the supplies used. If it was all cooked together, less fuel would be used and the supplies should last longer. I need volunteers to be placed in charge of a soup kitchen, to itemise the supplies we have, and to draw up some meal plans."

Everyone seemed to agree with this idea. Since the gas had stopped flowing a few days ago, people were finding it harder to cook and prepare food, and the gas barbeques that most people had switched to using were beginning to run out of gas. Russell, who lived down the road, came up with a great idea.

"If we use my large garden marquee, the cooking could be done outside. We haven't got a gas barbeque, so my family have been cooking on a fire pit I've constructed on our patio. I don't think it would be too hard for me to construct a larger one that would be suitable for cooking for all of us."

Pete thanked him and after asking if there were any objections, which there were not, told him to start immediately and to tell him if he needed any help at all. The cooking had reminded me to raise the issue about the water supply. I suggested that even though the water was still coming out of the taps, it would probably be a good idea to boil it first before drinking it. Pete thanked me and put it down on his list.

A couple of the neighbours were standing at the back, looking ill at ease throughout. Pete asked them if everything was OK and whether they had anything they wanted to add to the meeting.

John, one of the neighbours who had hidden the previous day at the first sign of trouble, stepped forward and spoke.

"Pete, we do appreciate what you and everybody else is doing for us, but a few of us are very uneasy about the whole concept of living in an armed camp. I hate the idea of guns being carried and used.

I've tried to learn to live with it and I know it's only being done to protect us, but after yesterday and the killing of all those people.

I've decided to leave and I think there are a few other families who'll want to join me."

"But John, where are you going to go? As far as we know, it's like this everywhere. You'll only be safe if you stay here!" Pete replied. "Your principles will most likely get you all killed. You heard what the gang that attacked us yesterday were doing! That's going to be happening everywhere. You won't stand a chance!" John stood his ground.

"I understand what you're saying, but I've made up my mind and we're going. There must be somewhere out there where we can live a civilised and normal life!" I stood there and listened, not saying a word, but thinking about them to myself.

I can see that the other three families who seem to be agreeing with John are also the ones who didn't help yesterday and I'm still pissed off with them. As far as I'm concerned, the way I feel now, if they don't want to cooperate and contribute, as the vast majority of the neighbours are doing, they may as well leave and go and look for this impossible place they think exists somewhere.

Pete asked for a few minutes to think, so we all stood around. A couple of people tried to persuade John and the others to change their minds, but they were unwavering in their determination to leave. Pete came back and asked for quiet.

"John, as you're obviously determined to go, I have a proposal. We'll give you as many supplies as you can carry, but in return you'll allow us to use your houses and anything left in them. Obviously if you do return, they'll be yours again."

John asked for a moment and he and the other families went off for a discussion. He returned and said, "That's fair, and we agree, but can we ask that if we put any personal items we can't carry, such as photos, paintings and family mementoes, into one room in each house, that you'll respect them and keep them safe?" It was a reasonable request and everyone was in agreement. They would leave as soon as they had everything sorted and had collected their supplies.

Once everyone had gone back to whatever task they were busy with, Allan and Pete walked over to me. Allan had asked for a couple of people to accompany him to the police station, to check firstly if the prisoners were OK, and to give them some food and water, and secondly, to help him start moving the supplies and equipment back to the road, as it would be easier if we could use my trailer.

Of course I agreed and went to get it from my garage as Pete rounded up a few more volunteers.

CHAPTER EIGHTEEN

We felt a bit safer leaving the road, given that the previous day we'd apparently eliminated the biggest threat to us in the area. We were all armed, but as we pushed the trailer the short distance up to the police station, we still cast nervous glances around, looking for a potential threat. Every house we passed appeared to be deserted. 'Where's everybody gone?' asked one of the men.

I gave it some thought.

"I think a lot of people have left for the countryside in the hope of finding food, but when I was driving around yesterday a few people came out of their houses as I passed, and then we had that confrontation with the group outside Jerry's house. I think there are more people than you think."

I paused.

"If some of them still have food, they're probably hiding away and trying to survive on their own, but as people get more desperate with every passing day, we'll come across more people either begging us for help or trying to take what we have by force. The one thing we can't afford to do is relax. I know I keep on about it, but we're in a 'life or death' situation and survival's going to be tough, even for people like us, who are well supplied at the moment."

I was beginning to feel like a survivalist prepping nutter, preaching to anyone who would listen, but I knew I was right and hoped that the more I went on about it, the more people would pay attention and understand. I probably didn't need to worry though; the gunfight we'd had yesterday must have made the situation we were in very real for the doubters.

We were greeted by carnage at the police station. As we walked into the cell area in the basement of the building, we could hear someone shouting for help through the solid cell door. Allan dropped the hatch in the door to see inside. Of the six men who had been locked up yesterday, four appeared to be dead and one was standing in a corner holding a knife towards the sixth man, who was built like a man mountain and was shouting for someone to help him. Allan gripped his shotgun, passed me the keys and asked me to unlock the door when he said so.

"Right. Move against the back wall, drop whatever weapons you've got, and face it with your hands on your heads." When they were in position, he indicated for me to open the door. I did as I was asked and stood out of the way as Allan entered the cell, holding his shotgun ready. The big bloke gave a sudden roar, pushed himself away from the wall, turned and lunged towards Allan.

Allan already had his gun aimed at him and pulled the trigger, half decapitating him, and sending him flying back against the wall. The other man screamed and crouched down against the wall, expecting the next shot to be aimed at him. Allan quickly passed his gun to me, grabbed him and cuffed his arms behind his back and dragged him out of the cell. We checked the others in the cell but they were all dead. They had been beaten to a pulp.

It took a while for the three of us to calm him down, so that he could tell us what had happened. Just before we had arrived, a fight had broken out over the last bottle of water that had been left for them. The big bloke had claimed it and the others had tried to take it from him. In the ensuing fight, he'd gone berserk, and even though it had been five to one, he'd overpowered them all and killed them with his bare hands.

It was only the fact that the survivor had a knife hidden on him that had saved his sorry life. He had been trying to hold him at bay for the last ten minutes. We locked him in another cell while we decided what to do with him.

Bob asked Allan if he was OK after what he'd just done.

"Weirdly I'm fine. I thought he was going to do it and after yesterday, I know that we're going to have to do things that only a few weeks ago, none of us in our worst nightmares would have imagined. But now it seems acceptable.

Does that sound weird to anyone?" No one disagreed. Yesterday seemed to have toughened us up.

We decided to delay the decision about the prisoner, because no harm could come to him on his own and we still had a lot of work to do. Allan walked us round the police station, identifying equipment he wanted to take with us. He showed us where all the food supplies were stored.

"That is a heck of a lot of food!" I said, stating the obvious, as we stared at the huge piles of boxes stacked in various rooms. "Why did so much get dropped here before the event?" I asked.

"I'm not sure," replied Allan, "I can only assume it was meant to be distributed around all the other stations, but due to some cockup they forgot to do it. When I met officers from other stations when we were still patrolling, most of them said they were running out of food. I suppose I'm glad I didn't start offering what I had around, because if I had, it would probably all be gone by now."

"Why is it still here?" I asked. "Surely the other officers based here would have come back to get it for themselves?"

"They would have done, but when they stopped reporting for duty they just took what supplies they could carry. I was bloody annoyed at them for forgetting their responsibilities. If they'd stayed and worked, they would still have been able to take food back to their families and carry out their duties. I thought, bugger them, and did a bit of lock changing on the main doors, so I knew I was the only one with a key to access the station. Without a stick of dynamite, you won't get through that front door without a key." Allan said, with a sly grin on his face.

We stood there for a minute, impressed by his cunning.

"Come on then mate, show us what to take first," I said. We worked out that it would probably take us at least a full day to move the enormous amount of food stored there. I was secretly very pleased, as following on from my thoughts of leaving yesterday, the amount of food we now had would feed us all for months, possibly longer, when it had all been sorted through. So for the moment, my fears and doubts about the long term future of our group were dispelled. Allan also showed us the riot gear that was stored at the station. There was a room full of bulletproof body armour vests, shields, batons and military-looking helmets.

He explained that, as part of his "head of security" duties, he planned to train as many of us as possible in crowd and riot control drills.

I know it sounds wrong, because most people in the country were suffering terribly at the moment, but I was beginning to feel excited about the future.

It all seemed to be working out better than in any of the scenarios I'd thought up during my years of planning and preparation.

Loading up the trailer for the first time, I talked to Allan about how we should go about rescuing the women who were being kept prisoner at the gang's house.

"I know, I've been thinking about it as well. I think that when we get back, we should leave a team of people to carry on moving the supplies. Then a few of us should go and have a look at where they're staying and see if any ideas come to mind."

We questioned the prisoner again. He was even more talkative today, now that we'd saved his life.

"There shouldn't be more than five or six people left at the house." Now he was eager to help us he explained, "They never keep a guard and only their leader, a guy named Malcolm, who is now dead, has been able to keep them under control. He organised the stealing and murdering to get supplies. If it had been up to most of us, we would have stayed in and got drunk and high, only thinking about going out when we ran out."

He thought that all the men with guns had been out with the gang, when they'd seen the Land Rover leave and decided to attack us. This was good news, as it looked as if we would be facing only five or six, drunk or high people, with little or no tactical awareness.

"What do we do with them if we capture them without a fight?" I asked Allan, who responded instantly.

"Since yesterday I've been giving it quite a lot of thought. As far as we know, there's no rule of law left and in my opinion, it's probably our duty to remove from what society we have left, anyone we think will continue to harm others. I'm not saying we hang anybody we don't like from the nearest tree.

We need to form some sort of jury to decide what should be done with them. Imagine if we let them go, because even if we knew what they'd done, we couldn't face killing them, and then we discovered that they'd moved to another area and carried on stealing, raping and murdering other people out there who were just trying to survive like us? How would we feel then? Hard decisions will have to be made for the good of everyone out there, not just us."

"I agree with you," I said, "but this needs to be discussed with everybody. We can't have people thinking we're taking the law into our own hands, (although of course, we would be), and thinking we're bloodthirsty murderers. People will need to agree, or at least understand, what we may have to do, or our group might fall apart because of disagreements about our conduct. As you know, I've been sort of preparing for an event like this for years and I've thought about a number of possible circumstances. The concept of acting like Judge Dredd is one that I have thought of." Allan chuckled at that thought.

"But if it's what we need to do to keep us and possibly other people safe, then it's a course of action I'd be prepared to take,"

I continued. "Whether I'll be able to take the life of someone who isn't directly threatening me at the time is something I'll have to think about, if and when it happens. As some of them got away yesterday, that gang at the house will know by now what happened. If they've got the intelligence to expect us to attack, we'll find out when we go for a recce. I'm half hoping they'll have just left, but the other half of me wants to punish them for what they've done," I added grimly. Allan nodded in agreement, as we finished loading the trailer and pushed it back.

CHAPTER NINETEEN

Pete agreed with our idea of scoping out the gang's house and we discussed the best people to take with us. Jerry was first on the list. If the gang was still there and we decided to try to rescue the women immediately, they might be in need of medical attention. Bob was next, as he was competent with a firearm and had handled himself well the day before. Alex and Jon had also done well, so we added them to the list. Pete called them together, told them what we were planning, and asked them if they would be willing to take part. They all agreed, so Pete told them to check with their respective wives, whether they would be happy for them to go. A clever ploy, that, because they'd be walking into a situation in which they could potentially be hurt or killed, and Pete wanted to be sure that anyone who might be affected by his decision was happy to take part, even if things went wrong.

The wives duly came over and asked Allan for more details.

"I'll be leading the operation and we'll be going to the police station to put on body armour and helmets, which will give us as much protection as possible. I can promise you that we'll only try to rescue the women if I think we can do it without putting any of us at an unacceptable amount of risk."

Somewhat mollified, they agreed that their husbands should go.

Jerry and I went back to my house to tell Becky and Fiona what we were planning. You could see the worry on their faces, but they agreed that we should go. They were happier when I told them that we would be wearing bulletproof vests and helmets. We gave our respective wives and children hugs and kisses, promised to be careful and left to find Allan. We took our walkie-talkies with us so that we could keep everyone informed of our progress.

Allan gathered us all together and we discussed tactics for the operation. First, we decided what weapons to take.

Jerry and I had our MP5s and pistols. Bob had taken charge of the shotguns we'd gathered from the gang the previous day, and had cleaned and checked them over. Alex and Jon were given two of those. Allan asked if he could use Jerry's pump-action shotgun. Bob distributed cartridges to Alex, Jon and Allan. Jerry and I made sure our magazines for the pistols and MP5s were fully loaded.

Allan's tactics were very simple.

"If we have to take the house by force, Jerry will stay back and guard the outside, while Tom and I lead the rest of us in trying to clear the house room by room. We've all seen house clearances carried out by Special Forces on television shows. Our plan is a simple formation to follow, so that we'll all be covering each other and not getting in each other's line of fire."

"Why do I have to stay outside?" Jerry asked.

"You're the only doctor we have, you'll be needed to treat any injured among us and if you get hurt, who would help you?" Nobody could argue with this. I pointed out something that had occurred to me about our firearms.

"It might be better to use the MP5s and pistols in the house. If we start shooting with shotguns, with their spread of shot, we might accidentally harm the women we're there to rescue." Jerry responded to that one quickly.

"Right, Tom, I'll give Allan my MP5, and we'll give Alex and Jon our pistols." Jerry and I then gave them all a five-minute demonstration on firing and loading them. Bob kept his shotgun, saying he would act as heavy backup and only fire if absolutely necessary.

We must have looked terrifying as the six of us walked through Moseley, heavily armed and wearing full body armour, with helmets and leg and arm protectors on as well.

As we walked towards St Agnes Road, we tried to identify which houses still looked occupied. Allan was planning a local census to identify possible future threats, and also to find people we might be able to offer help to if possible. About fifteen or so houses still looked as if there were people in them, but we didn't stop to check. We made a mental note of them and carried on to our destination.

The house was one of the largest on the road, set well back behind an "in and out" drive, with plenty of bushes and trees to hide it from passing cars and pedestrians. I knew the house, because the owners had been friends with people we knew, and we'd often admired it (with a hint of jealousy) when passing. I couldn't remember their names, but knew they'd had four young children. My anger increased, knowing they'd probably all been killed just for having one of the best houses on the road. Hiding in the bushes, we took up a position where we could get a good look at the property.

One of them was sitting outside on an armchair, swigging from a bottle. He must have been some sort of lookout or sentry, but he seemed far more interested in drinking from his bottle and looking at the magazine he was holding. Another man came out and urinated in the bushes by the front door. He looked a bit unsteady on his feet. The rest of the house seemed quiet. Allan indicated that we should move back a bit.

It was quite hard to move quietly through the bushes, but luckily it was a windy day, so our slightly noisy attempts at stealth were drowned out by the bushes and trees swaying and rustling in the wind.

Allan whispered, "I know we only came for a recce, but I think we should try to rescue the women now. Does anyone disagree?" We all shook our heads, so he continued.

"As we can see, there's one on sentry duty, but we don't know how many more are inside, apart from the one who came out for a piss. I don't think they have any guns, because surely, if they did, the one on guard would have one, and the other one we saw wasn't carrying a weapon. I think we should take out the guard and then attack the house. We don't know where they are in the house, so if we stick to our formation and are as loud and aggressive as possible, hopefully, that will shock and intimidate them and stop them organising some sort of defence.

"There are a lot of rooms in a house this large so be prepared for them to be coming at us from anywhere. The ones we've seen look either drunk or high, and that'll slow them down, but it could also make them unpredictable, so get ready for anything. If they're coming towards us, take them down. If they're running away it's up to you what you do, but remember what these guys have been doing. These men are murderers and rapists.

Personally, I'm not feeling very sympathetic towards them at the moment, but you do what you think is best and no one here will judge you for it." We checked our weapons and made sure we knew where our spare magazines were.

"Right, this is it, boys. Let's get this over with," I whispered, as we crept back through the bushes. Jerry positioned himself behind a large tree and pointed his weapon towards the house. The guy in the chair by the front door was still drinking from his bottle as Allan crept from the cover of the bushes and dropped to one knee, raised his weapon and took aim.

The man noticed him, stood up and raised his baseball bat.

He looked as if he was about to shout a warning as Allan's silenced weapon killed him with three bullets to the chest. We rushed towards the house, forming a square, with Allan and me in the lead, holding our MP5s ready, and Alex, Jon and Bob to the rear, with their pistols pointed over our shoulders and Bob's shotgun pointed at the sky. As we entered the house we all shouted as Allan had instructed us,

"Police! Nobody move!" over and over. As we entered a room off the hallway, a door burst open upstairs and a man started to run down the stairs. Alex raised his pistol and fired twice and the man crumpled and fell, sliding the rest of the way down the steps.

The adrenaline was pumping and our shouting, as well as intimidating those in the house, was keeping us fired up.

There was no one in the first two rooms downstairs, but as we entered the kitchen area another man ran towards us out of another room, holding a large kitchen knife.

I dropped him with a burst from my gun. A scream from behind the island unit in the kitchen made us all turn and point our guns towards it. Allan shouted to whoever was there, not to move and to lie on the floor.

Allan and I moved quickly around the kitchen with guns pointed towards the island, fingers on triggers. Alex, Jon and Bob, I noticed, had turned and were keeping their guns pointed towards the doors leading into the kitchen. Hiding behind the island, lying on the floor, were three women. The older one had her arms protectively over the other two. Allan shouted at them.

"Don't move! We're here to rescue you. How many men are in the house and where are they?' The woman in the middle looked up at us, terror showing in her eyes. I recognised her. "Michelle? Is that you?" I asked. "It's Tom, Jane's brother." All she could do was nod. I didn't know her that well, but she was a good friend of my sister. She had divorced her husband the previous year when she'd discovered he was having an affair with someone at work.

Unable to have any children, she'd been left completely alone, and my sister had been her shoulder to cry on initially, and more recently had been acting as a matchmaker, trying to fix her up with other single friends. She was a very pretty woman in her mid-thirties and I'd got into trouble with Becky once by remarking on how attractive she was, and how any man would be lucky to go out with her. I know you don't have to tell me where I went wrong with that statement, because Becky spent a good two hours putting me straight.

I moved closer and crouched next to her, saying quietly, "Look, we're here to help you, we're the ones who killed the rest of them yesterday when they attacked us. I need you to tell me where the rest of them are and then we can get you to a safe place." She still looked shocked, but you could see the relief flow through her when she realised we were a rescue party. Trembling slightly, she tried to collect herself.

"There are six of them here. After yesterday all they've done is get drunk and high."

"Have they got any guns?" I asked quickly.

She shook her head, sobbing, "No, I don't think so."

"Are there any more women in the house?" I asked.

"No, not any more, they killed the other two yesterday when they tried to escape." We all looked at each other.

"Bastards!" said Jon. "Let's get them."

Allan, who was standing close by, took charge again.

"You three stay there and don't move!" Then addressing the five of us, he said, "Right, let's keep moving, Bob you stay here and guard the ladies. There are three of those bastards left. We'll clear the ground floor first and then move upstairs. Stay sharp, they may not have guns but you never know what they'll do."

We moved through the downstairs rooms in the house. They were empty, but all the rooms had been trashed, with rubbish and empty bottles everywhere. Allan held a finger to his lips to indicate for us to be quiet. In the silence, we could hear footsteps and banging coming from upstairs. It sounded like furniture being dragged across a floor.

Allan motioned for us to follow him, but to be quiet. We crept up the stairs, guns pointing in all directions. A figure suddenly darted from one room and ran along the landing. He was heading away from Allan and me, but Alex and Jon, who were following us up the stairs and walking backwards to cover our rear, were looking straight at him as he ran across the gallery. They both shot twice, the figure let out a scream then crumpled to the floor and didn't move. The rest of the rooms were clear, apart from one. Its door was closed and when we tried to kick it in it didn't give.

"The last two spineless arseholes have barricaded themselves in," said Allan. "Come out, you bastards and face some real men, not the women and children you're used to raping and killing!" he shouted through the door.

"Oh that'll make 'em want to," I said sarcastically.

"Well I'm not going to beg them, am I!" replied Allan. "In fact, you know what, we haven't got time for this," he said furiously. He clicked the rate of fire selector on his gun to full auto, told us to stand back, aimed it at the door and emptied the magazine through it. There was the sound of breaking glass and a scream, followed by a thud outside. I ran to the landing window that overlooked the front, and saw a body lying on the drive. Allan gave a few mighty kicks to the door, which moved the table that had been hastily dragged up against it, and shoulder barged the door open.

The other man was lying dead on the floor, having been hit many times by Allan's wild shooting through the closed door.

The one outside, in his desperation to escape, had apparently dived straight through the window. A twenty-foot fall head first onto the brick drive had taken care of him.

Allan immediately got back to business. "All four of us stay in formation, let's do one more sweep of the house to make sure they've all gone, and then we can get Jerry in here to take care of the women." Five minutes later he gave the house the all-clear and told Jon to get Jerry inside. In the kitchen, the three women were obviously still in shock and extremely distressed. Michelle was the most composed and was comforting the other two, who looked to be in their late teens or early twenties. Jerry gave them each a quick examination to check for any obvious injuries but it was the damage inside, the mental trauma they'd all experienced, which was going to be the real problem. We couldn't imagine what these poor women had gone through or been made to do during their captivity. They would recover, but it was going to be a long and difficult healing process that would need careful handling.

While Jerry was attending to the women, I hung around in the kitchen, trying to be a familiar face, and offering words of comfort to Michelle. Allan, Jon, Alex and Bob conducted a search of the house. We'd seen food and other supplies scattered around during our search, but hadn't been paying much attention to it.

Allan came up to me and said quietly, "Bloody hell mate, there's loads of stuff here. It looks like these were the boys that emptied the local supermarkets and I can't begin to guess how many houses they've robbed. We need to sort through it and get it back to the road. It'll keep us going for ages."

That reminded me to call Becky on the radio to tell her we were all fine and unhurt. You could hear the relief in her voice. They had all panicked when they'd heard distant shots and had been going crazy with worry. I assured her that we were all fine and that we'd rescued three women. I told her that Michelle was one of them, and promised to call her when we were on our way back.

I asked her to put Pete on the radio and told him about the supplies we'd discovered.

I suggested that he start planning how to get them back to the road, so that we could discuss it when we got home.

Jerry, with his gentle manner and kind words, had managed to calm the women down. He kept assuring them that they were all safe and would be taken good care of. The younger women introduced themselves as Kim and Mandy. They started to ask questions about why we'd come to help them, but Jerry said there would be time for all that later.

What was important right now was to get them safely back. Michelle, Kim and Mandy assured us that they would be OK to walk back. I asked them if they had anything they wanted to take with them before we left. Michelle answered for all of them when she said bitterly,

"You can burn this place down for all I care, there's been too much evil in this house." There was no answer to that so we all left. I radioed Becky and told her to expect us in ten minutes.

CHAPTER TWENTY

Back at the road, Becky and the other women immediately took charge of Michelle, Kim and Mandy. Becky had organised for lots of hot water to be heated up, so they could at least have a shower and get clean. This would be an important first step in their recovery process, making them at least feel human again. The rescue party went outside to find Pete. We were immediately surrounded by everyone else on the road, all wanting to know the details of our mission. Allan gave them a brief summary, mentioning that not one of the gang had survived our assault. No one seemed upset about this and most congratulated us on getting rid of "that scum". Then he embarrassed us by singing our praises and saying how well we'd worked as a team, after such a short training and planning period. Looking back, we realised that it had gone amazingly well; not one of us had even come close to being hurt and we'd worked together to achieve our aims.

More importantly, we'd struck up a bond which would help us in the pursuit of our main goal, survival.

Pete brought us back to the present.

"Can we have bit of quiet, please? While you were gone, John and the other two families left. They collected as many supplies as they could carry and just walked quietly up the street and out of our lives.

Retrieval of the supplies from the police station is going well and I'm storing it all in the front room of our house, where it's being recorded and catalogued. Tell me again about how much you found at the gang's house."

When we told him how much there was, it was unanimously agreed that we would stop collecting the supplies from the police station, and lock it up where it would be secure. Then we would start making trips to St Agnes Road to collect everything we could from there.

Allan was focusing on security on the road.

"I need a few men so that we can continue to secure our perimeter. We've had so much to do that allocating manpower is becoming a problem. There are seventeen families still on the road, and we need at least two people on each barricade at all times to keep a look out." Pete said,

"I also want to allocate six men to collect the food from the gang's house. Allan wants at least three or four to help him. With my arm in plaster, I can't do much, apart from organising us all for the moment, so it doesn't leave many to help with the defence of the road, should we need it."

Bob had been giving it some thought.

"Couldn't we use some of the older children as extra manpower? They've been having a great time, playing in the road and generally treating this as an extended holiday, but there's no school in sight at the end of it, and boredom's been setting in recently, and now they're starting to get under people's feet."

He paused, swallowing.

"I know that after the events of yesterday, the smaller children are being kept inside. If we have another crisis, they'll need to be found quickly for their own protection, and we can't afford to have parents running around, trying to find them, just when they'll be needed to help defend the road."

It was a long speech for Bob, and needed consideration.

Pete thought about this for a while and decided that our first priority was security. He addressed all the parents standing around him.

"Would you be willing to let your older children help Allan and the others? Every group would have at least one of the walkie-talkies that Tom's provided, so they'd be able to keep in touch with each other, and could be recalled at the first sign of trouble?"

They all agreed and most of the women volunteered to help as well.

Pete, obviously embarrassed, apologised for being such an old timer and admitted that he'd only considered the men for the heavy work but of course, if they wanted to help and felt up to it, they would be more than welcome.

Twelve excited children ranging from seventeen to ten were gathered up and told to report to Pete, where they would be given new duties. Pete gave them all a stern lecture on listening to their elders and doing exactly what they were told. They were being trusted to help, and must not abuse that trust by messing about. You could see their parents standing at the back, grinning wryly, as the children listened intently to everything that was said. There were few comments from them such as "Bloody hell, he hasn't listened to a word I've told him for years, all he does is grunt, and a few lines from General Pete over there and he looks like a model citizen. Amazing!"

Pete gave Allan eight of the bigger children, as most of the work he had would be physical. He soon had them hard at work, pushing cars out of the way to clear the view up and down the road, or positioning them to help strengthen the barricades. The younger children were put to work moving the supplies around and helping Pete compile a list of what we had.

Pete sent a group of ten, (five men, me included, and five women), up to the gang's house with my trailer, to start moving supplies. One of the women had the bright idea of bringing rucksacks and shopping trolleys or wheelbarrows with us, so that we could bring more back with every trip. A quick trip up to the supermarket on the High Street revealed plenty of abandoned trolleys, so we picked those up on the way past. On the way to the house we agreed on the following procedure: It would take at least four or five people to push the fully loaded trailer back to the road. While the rest were pushing the trailer or shopping trolleys, three of us would stay and move the supplies on to the drive. This would speed up the process of loading the trailer and trolleys when they returned. At the house, nobody commented on the bodies outside or inside, we all just got on with moving the supplies. It was an exhausting day, but we managed six trips back and forth to the house before the ten of us wearily trudged home in the growing dusk, five pushing the trailer and five pushing trolleys, and each of us weighed down by a full rucksack on our backs. There was still more to collect, but it would have to wait until the morning.

At home, Becky reported that Michelle and the girls were doing well. Jerry had given them all a sedative and they were sleeping soundly in one of the spare rooms. They hadn't wanted to be separated and were all sharing the same bed. They had told Becky some of the things they had been made to do and she had been horrified. She wouldn't give me any details, saying it was their story to tell if they chose to, but we had definitely done the right thing in killing those men. For Becky, with her liberal views on prisons and capital punishment, to come out with a statement like that was quite something.

I made no comment on that, but just told her I loved her for always doing the right thing and wanting to help people.

Russell was still working on his wood-burning oven concept, but in the meantime he had rigged up his marquee in the road and was using camping stoves and barbecues for cooking the meals. The volunteer cooks had made a lovely smelling stew. The church hall at the top of the road had yielded some very large pans, which were put to good use. We stood in line to get dinner and returned home to eat. As I hadn't seen much of Stanley and Daisy since the attack, I spent some time playing with them before tucking them up in bed, and read them both a bedtime story.

Allan came round to see how the women we had rescued were doing. Becky briefed him while I opened a few cans of beer for Jerry, Allan and myself and a bottle of wine for Becky and Fiona. I still had quite a stock of drink in the house, and with the amount we'd retrieved from the gang's house, it was one thing we were definitely not going to run out of soon.

I asked Allan how his defences were going and he said that he was coming up with new ideas all the time. I thought about the materials I'd bought.

"Before this all kicked off, I bought a load of mesh, and I'd planned to cover my windows with it, in the hope that it would make the house more resistant to attack. I've got quite a large stock of barbed and razor wire which I'll be happy to let you use." Allan was excited to hear this.

"That would make my plans easier. My idea, based on the speech you made to the neighbours the other day, was to create a ring of defence around all of the houses. I plan to raise the fence line, by taking fence panels from between the properties and attaching them to the existing panels to create a high wall. If I could use the barbed and razor wire as well, it would make them harder to climb over."

"Right then, let's talk about it some more in the morning, when I can show you how much stuff I've collected over the years. I've also had some ideas I can tell you about, because protecting my property is something I've given a lot of thought to over the years."

Pete had popped in to see Jerry, wanting some stronger painkillers for his arm, which was aching badly after the day's exertions.

"I haven't finished cataloguing all the supplies we've got yet, but once that's done, I'm planning to work out with our volunteer cooks just how many meals we can provide and how long it will all last."

That led to a discussion about how to extend what we had by foraging for food from vegetable gardens in the area. I thought I could help there.

"I've got pages of information about wild edible plants and berries which will be useful for finding fresh food for the group. Moseley Park, at the end of my garden, has a fishing lake, so we might be able to catch fish, and then there are the ducks and the geese on the lake which could go into the pot as well."

As so many ideas had been put forward, all with their own merits, it was going to be impossible to act on them all at once. We agreed that Pete would write them all up in a list, in order of importance. The list would probably change on a daily basis, as tasks were completed or new ideas were thought of which might take precedence, but at least it was a start.

We'd only built the barricade of cars the day before and so much had happened since then, it was all a bit hard to take in, but it was important to recognise what we'd achieved as well. We'd survived a violent attack and defended ourselves successfully, we'd rescued the women from the gang by attacking them ourselves, and we'd collected an enormous amount of food and still had more to get. Everyone was working amazingly well together, and with Pete's organisational skills, allocating the available workforce to get through his ever-growing list of jobs, I was sure that every day we would be in a better position to survive. Pete wanted us to be even more organised, and suggested that the morning meeting should become a regular event. If we combined it with eating our breakfast, cooked in the communal kitchen, the day's work could be allocated to individuals or groups, and it would also be an opportunity for anyone to raise concerns, or add another idea to be discussed.

Becky and I questioned whether it would it be fair for us to share the communal food, when we had enough of our own. We didn't want it to appear as if we were hoarding our own stuff and using up valuable supplies that other people could use. Jerry and Fiona agreed with us.

Pete, always one step ahead, it seemed, had already thought we would object to it, so explained his reasoning, "I think it would be better for the group if you ate the same meals as the rest of us. That would prevent any bad feeling due to people thinking you were eating better than them. If you donate the equivalent of what you eat back to the group, then that way there can be no accusations."

"Are you some sort of Machiavellian genius?" I replied laughing, "You're always one step ahead of everybody. Does your brain ever stop thinking? Not only have you persuaded a large group of independent and strong-willed people to co-operate, but now you're second guessing us all! How do you do it?"

He gave me a wink and said, "I suppose it just comes naturally to some people. But seriously, Tom, I don't think you can begin to appreciate how thankful we all are for what you've done for us. If it wasn't for you, we'd all be starving to death, or we'd have been killed by that gang, or others, out there. You knew what had happened and warned us. You made us build that barricade, and it was that and your guns that saved our lives the other day." He stepped closer and placed a hand on my shoulder.

It was you that befriended Allan and Jerry, and look what they've brought to the group. In short, we all owe you our lives, and I think we'll continue to rely on you in the future.

Look, not two minutes ago you told us about all the stuff you've got to help Allan improve our defences. I may be the nominated leader of us all, but I still look to you for advice and guidance. I'm just the man who's good at organising."

I was very embarrassed by his little speech. I'd just been doing what I thought was the right thing, and hadn't expected any recognition. All I'd wanted was to protect my family. I grunted a reply of thanks and felt myself going bright red, while everybody smiled at my discomfort. Later that night, cuddling up with Becky in bed, she teased me mercilessly and called me her saviour and hero.

CHAPTER TWENTY-ONE

At the morning meeting, over porridge and coffee, Pete allocated our daily tasks. Priority was to be given to improving our defences. He organised one group to send to the gang's house to finish collecting the supplies, and then to carry on collecting from the police station, and another group to man the barricades. Every other available man, woman and child, was allocated to Allan to help him. Allan gave me joint responsibility, as I had more experience in construction, and even though we agreed on what needed to be done, he knew I would be better able to work out how to do it.

While Allan concentrated on working in the back gardens, raising the height of the fence panels, I started the defences on the road. We had the barricades of cars at either end, but I wanted to improve the defensive line where our houses were. By now, everybody had moved into the ten central houses surrounding mine, five on either side of the road.

Initially I created a fence line, using the fence posts and post-fix concrete I'd bought from the builders' merchant. I marked where I wanted the holes dug and the teams soon had them finished and the posts in the holes.

Quick drying post-fix mix doesn't take long to harden, and while everybody nailed strands of barbed wire and then coils of razor wire to the top and bottom, I got on with making gates for both fences. I made one wide enough to walk through, so that people could pass through to man the barricade at the bottom of the road, but for the fence facing the High Street I made the gate wide enough to drive cars through. The fence wasn't straight and it certainly wasn't a thing of beauty, but it would provide a very effective way of keeping unwanted people out.

My next plan would be to construct a solid barrier behind the wire fence to protect us in the event of another attack. I just needed to think of the best way to do it without using all the plywood sheets I had.

Pete kept rotating the workers every hour, giving people a rest while they kept watch on the barricades. After just two days of hard work, Allan and I both agreed that what we had created should, hopefully, be good enough to protect us. We were surrounded by a high fence topped with barbed wire or razor wire. Long nails had been hammered through the fences to further deter people from trying to climb over them. Stanley had come up with the idea of attaching tin cans to the wire. They would rattle together and make a noise to warn us of an attempt by anyone to climb the fences.

Without the usual traffic noises you hear in a city, it was eerily quiet at night, so any sound would easily be heard. The wire mesh I had provided covered most of the downstairs windows of the houses. Vulnerable doors and windows had been boarded up with plywood. On the road, we had the barricades of cars at each end, and a barbed and razor wire fence across the road where our houses were. I had the idea of using bulk bags filled with soil to build a solid wall inside the wire fence, to protect us further. A few trips to the local builders' merchant provided us with enough empty bags, and the wall was rapidly being completed by a hoard of enthusiastic children, armed with wheelbarrows and buckets and spades, as they dug up the soil from front gardens on the road and filled the bulk bags.

My house, being the most central in the road, was designated as a shelter where, in the event of an attack, anyone not involved in the fighting would gather together.

The doors were reinforced with more plywood and we made simple wooden locking bars, which could be dropped into place to bar them completely. Allan also planned to build more defensive positions in the back gardens and close to the barricades, to provide protection from bullets, or whatever missiles might be thrown at us in the event of an attack.

Finally, he was devising a signalling system using whistles, so that people would know which direction the attack was coming from, and react accordingly.

None of it was very pretty but it all seemed very effective. It was amazing how much could be achieved in a short space of time, with everybody working together as a team.

All the food had been collected from the police station and the gang's house. Pete had been calculating the stores, with our newly acquired stock.

"I've worked out that we now have enough to feed us all for over six months. This is great, but it will still run out eventually, so now that most of the defensive work has been done, we'll need to carry out foraging missions to collect what we can from empty houses and shops."

Pete proposed this at the next breakfast meeting, telling them,

"Allan will continue his work on the defences, but the majority of this work has been done now, so I'll need to allocate more people to supply gathering."

"Then you'd better take some women on those trips, because if it's left to you men, most of you can't even find your own socks in the sock drawer, so I despair at what you'll find," Becky said, causing much hilarity.

Pete, once he had stopped laughing, was in full agreement, so despite the mock disgust and outrage from the men, a least one woman was allocated to lead each foraging party.

Pete then made a number of other suggestions, to which we all agreed.

"If a house looks occupied, we won't try to force entry, we'll try to communicate with whoever's inside, reassuring them that we mean them no harm. If they want to talk to us and they prove to be friendly, we'll make it clear that we're not in a position to give out our own supplies, but that we'll be happy to offer any medical assistance we can, and help them improve their home defences.

If they want to join our foraging parties, then they'll be allocated a share of whatever we find. It seems to me the fairest way to do it. We're not animals, and if people need help, we'll offer what we can, but we still have to look after our own families. We can't afford to give away food we'll need ourselves, but if they want to help us find it, then they can have some." Everybody thought this was a fair plan, so Pete continued.

"If the people we meet turn out to be hostile, we'll just walk away and let them get on with trying to survive.

If we're attacked, all the foraging parties will be armed, so we'll respond with force and kill them if we have to, or at least take whatever weapons they've got, so that they won't be able to go on terrorising other people in the neighbourhood." Again, this met with agreement.

"If we meet other groups of people looking for supplies, the same rules will apply. If they're friendly, we'll try to work with them, or at least agree on areas to search so that we aren't wasting time searching properties and shops that have already been thoroughly cleared. We don't want to start getting into disputes over territory, and I hope that the majority of people we encounter will just be trying to survive, and will be happy to agree to work together, or at least to stay out of each other's way. If that isn't the case, then we'll do whatever is necessary to protect ourselves. All groups will carry walkie-talkies with them so that they can call for assistance if needed." Allan had something to add at this point.

"I think it would be a good idea for the response team to use pedal bikes to enable them to get to wherever they're needed more quickly. I'll train everybody who'll be going out, on the basics of working as a team, if attacked. We learned a valuable lesson in our assault on the gang's house, of how effective it was working together, and providing cover for each other.

Some simple instructions now could save lives, so I think we need to put this training in place." Pete replied to this.

"I couldn't agree more. Bob, can you and the rest of the team who attacked the gang's house carry on with the defences? In the meantime, Allan and Tom are going to give arms training."

Allan and I gave everyone else a crash course on safe gun handling and defensive techniques. We were mostly making it up as we went along, but as the day wore on, we learned a lot by trying to visualise all the different scenarios in which an attack might take place, and the best ways to counter them.

Everyone in a foraging party would be wearing police body armour and helmets for protection. For those who hadn't fired a shotgun before, I drew the outline of a person, with paint, on a shed in the back garden of one of the abandoned houses, and they all had some practice in taking a few shots at the target.

The training lasted for a couple of days, until Allan deemed everybody competent enough to go on foraging missions.

CHAPTER TWENTY-TWO

Russell unveiled his new wood burning oven. It was an incredible contraption, made from steel sheets and parts cannibalised from other ovens and barbecues. It had a large oven, heated from below by a wood fire, and a hotplate for heating pans on the side, also heated by a wood fire. He told us a bit about it,

"The only thing is, it only seems to have two heat settings: very hot and cold, but by trial and error, using different quantities of wood, I'm confident we'll learn how to use it properly."

It was very heavy and it took eight of us to manhandle it out of his garage and put it in the communal kitchen. We all stood around expectantly as Russell stacked the kindling and larger logs and lit the fires. A lot of smoke leaked out of the gaps and joints, but most went up the chimney. The mood was light, we knew it was another thing that we had achieved as a group.

Yes, we took the mickey out of Russell, telling him well done, but how was anybody going to see through all that smoke to cook? And various other witty remarks but he took it in good heart and pointed out,

"Well, if I'd had power, I could have used my welder to make better joints. You'll have to put up with it until I can think of a way to seal them."

"But Russ," I said, "your welder's been fried in the EMP, it wouldn't work anyway.

"It should. After what you told us, I read about EMPs in a back copy of one of the science journals I collect, and I reckon it'd be OK. I keep it in a steel tool safe along with all my other power tools, and, because I look after my tools, unlike the rest of you heathens, I lined it with rubber to stop them getting scratched. If a fuse has blown on it or something else has gone, I love tinkering with electronics, and I've got boxes and boxes of spares, so I would have been able to cobble something together and get it going. But I haven't bothered, because with no power, what's the point?"

I stood there looking at him, open-mouthed and shocked at my own stupidity. Eventually I said quietly,

"Would a four KVA generator power your welder? Because if it does, I've only bloody got one which should work. I haven't tested it yet, but I kept in in a Faraday cage, and it's only a pull start, so I reckon it should be OK."

He nodded.

I turned to Pete and said, "Pete, we've missed a trick here. I didn't know what Russ had and, yes, he's made something fantastic, but how much better would it have been if he could have used his tools? I feel so stupid!" I was angry with myself for overlooking the obvious.

As neighbours, we all knew each other to some extent, some a lot better than others, but in Russ's case I only had a vague idea of what he did.

He was some sort of consultant who had travelled a lot and had sometimes been away for long periods. "Russ," I said, "what exactly do you do?"

"My background's in engineering, but I specialise in helping to design and oversee the construction of power plants all over the world, and lately I've been doing mainly alternative energy projects, wind farms, tidal, projects like that. But my love is electronics, restoring old things and getting them working again, or making stuff from scratch, just to see if I can do it. Sometimes I have a month or two between projects and it gives me something to do. If I'd known about your generator, I could have made something a lot better than this thing."

Pete spoke up. "Look, no one is to blame here, we've achieved so much in such a short time, but Tom, you're right, we've all assumed that we know each other and what kind of skills we can bring to the group. Russ, I've known you for years, but I didn't know anything about you tinkering with electronics and stuff. I'm going to talk to everybody individually over the next day or so, and find out exactly what skills they have and if we can use them. But right now, I'm hungry, so let's see what our cooks can conjure up on the beast over there."

After a breakfast of pancakes and porridge, while Pete was organising the first foraging party and agreeing a route to take and a time limit for returning, I took Russ to my garage to show him my generator and tools. Allan and a few others went to the police station to feed the prisoner. We hadn't reached a decision yet about what to do with him. We'd all calmed down after the attack, and executing the man didn't hold much appeal for us, especially after Michelle spoke up for him.

"He was the only decent one in the gang. He never attacked or tried to force himself on me or the other girls, and one time, he tried to stop another girl being beaten to death by another gang member. I think he only joined them as a way of finding food and a chance to survive." Clearly, when Allan returned, we'd need to decide his fate.

Russell got the generator going at the first attempt, and we carried it to the kitchen, where once the oven had cooled down, he was planning to improve on his design. Pete informed him that he'd decided to make him our technology expert and tasked him with coming up with ideas to make our lives safer and, if possible, more comfortable. You could see the excitement in his eyes and the cogs in his brain ticking over. He quickly blurted out ideas about lighting and water filtration. Pete stopped him.

"Russ, finish the oven and then just check what everybody else has lying around. If you think you can use it and make something work, just come and tell me. You know what our priorities are and I'm sure with your ingenuity you'll be great. Just don't baffle me with science, tell me what it does and if it'll work."

By now, Allan had returned from the police station, so I reminded Pete that we needed to make a decision about the prisoner. He called everybody available together to discuss what we should do.

I spoke first. I didn't defend him, but I did explain what Michelle had told me about him. Allan spoke next, saying that he agreed with Michelle's opinion of the young man and that he didn't think he posed a risk to us at all. A few of them still wanted to put him on trial for murder and for all the horrible acts the gang had committed.

Pete handled the meeting well and listened to all the views and points made. He reminded everybody that if the vote found him guilty, we would have to execute him by hanging or firing squad and he would ask for volunteers from those giving the guilty verdicts, to carry out the sentence.

Pete explained he would be asking for two decisions by a show of hands: guilty or not guilty.

If he was found not guilty, the man would be set free, but with the promise that if we came across him at any point in the future, his sentence would be changed back to guilty. It was obvious from the vote that no one really had the heart or will for an execution, so most people voted "not guilty". Most seemed relieved about the result. There had been enough bloodshed and the idea of a public execution was too much.

I accompanied Allan up to the police station to release the prisoner. We both agreed that the right choice had been made and were as relieved as everyone else about not having to execute him.

He was overjoyed, but very scared about what he would face out there. Allan warned him about what would happen if we saw him again, handed him a small bag of food and told him to go. We watched as he ran up the road and disappeared around the corner.

While we were there we carried out another search in case we'd missed anything that might be useful. We found a few more sets of body armour and some cans of pepper spray, but the best find was the supplies for the vending machine, which we discovered after breaking open a locked cupboard. The chocolates and crisps would make great treats for the children. We both felt like Santa, as we each carried back two bin bags of goodies slung over our shoulders.

CHAPTER TWENTY-THREE

Pete was waiting for us to return before he sent out the first foraging party. I was tasked with leading the response team if they needed help. I'd wanted to be on the foraging party, but Pete had had a quiet word with me, saying that I had done enough lately and other members of our group needed to start doing things on their own, rather than relying on Allan, me or him to take the lead in everything. Also, although he was allocating everybody tasks on a daily basis, some people had more usable skills than others. Going on a foraging expedition was something everyone could contribute towards. Once again the ideas, when he put them forward, seemed obvious, but he was always the first one to come up with them.

Before they left, we reminded them to stick to the agreed route, and to keep checking in with us every ten minutes so that we could track their progress.

If we needed to rush over there to help them, we would know exactly where they were and there would be no delay in reaching them.

I checked on the kids. They were still working away at filling the bulk bags with soil.

They were all filthy but happy, and with a bit of adult encouragement, it had turned into a competition to see which group of children did more in a day, with the winners being allowed to pick the DVD to watch in the evening. The wall had a row of two bulk bags stacked on top of each other and one behind it to act as a walkway. It was going to be a solid barrier over 6ft high with the only weak point being the gate.

Allan had returned from making sure his team of workers were continuing the defences in the back gardens, and was trying to design a gate that would be solid enough to match the wall, but could be opened without too much effort. I told him to have a chat with Russell and see if they could come up with something using his welder. They were soon sitting at a table having a lively discussion about it.

I went home to catch up with Becky, and found her sitting at the kitchen table with Fiona, Michelle, Kim and Mandy. They seemed to be having a group counselling session, helping the women to adjust to their freedom and get over the horrors they had experienced. Not wanting to intrude, I grabbed a quick cup of coffee and left to find Pete and Jerry.

Jerry was finalising his list of residents of the road. He wanted to give everyone a complete health check and start regularly monitoring us all, in the hope that he would spot any health problems early and if possible, prevent them from becoming serious.

He said that Fiona was going to do the same with our teeth. Prevention would be better than cure and as Jerry and Fiona were the experts, Pete was giving them all the help he could so that they could start as soon as possible.

The foraging party had checked in a few times. They were having a few successes and were finding food in most of the empty houses, hidden in the back of cupboards or, using the torches I'd given them, in cellars. They had also seen some terrible things. In a few houses, they'd discovered people who had apparently starved to death in their beds. You could tell from their voices that it had been a harrowing experience, discovering people who had been too afraid to leave their houses to find help, and then when it was too late, not having the energy to move.

Most had probably gone to bed to try to keep warm and then died. In another house a whole family had committed suicide. A note had been left saying that they were overdosing on sleeping tablets, rather than face slowly starving to death. The smell from all the decomposing corpses had been horrendous and you knew if there were any dead bodies in a house as soon as you opened the door. After the first few dreadful discoveries, as soon as the front door was opened and the smell of death was released, they didn't enter the house. Instead, the front door was marked with a cross and the foraging party moved on.

They had encountered only one occupied house. The man had been unwilling to open the door, but had spoken to them out of an upstairs window. He claimed that he had enough food, as they had been preparing for years for an event like this, so when the event had happened he and his family had secured their house and sat tight. A few people had tried to break in, but had failed to gain entry, so he hadn't had to use any of his weapons. He had thanked them for the offer of medical help, but hadn't wanted to go foraging for supplies as he had enough. It was agreed that as the house was reasonably close to our road, we would check on them whenever a foraging party was passing, in case they needed any help.

CHAPTER TWENTY-FOUR

Over the next week or so, the community settled down to a routine. Allan announced that his defences were as good as he could make them, and gave the whole community the grand tour. Most of us had assisted in building them and I had helped Allan design and build a few of the features, but this was the first time most people had had the theory behind it all explained. We were surrounded by a sturdy high fence, bristling with nails and barbed wire. Fortified positions had been created and trees and bushes cut down and removed to create open spaces and remove hiding places for attackers. In the road we had three layers of defence: the barricades of cars, the wire fence and finally, the solid barrier of bulk bags, with a hinged metal gate made by Russell from car bonnets. Wooden planks had been laid to make a walkway on the bulk bags.

It was all very impressive and gave us the look of a frontier fort, with soldiers huddling behind the barricades, waiting for the next onslaught from hostile natives.

But so far we had not been tested again. A few people, either singly, or in groups, had been spotted, but as yet no one had approached us. Most of the community were starting to relax, thinking that the worst was over.

Realising this, Allan kept up his training schedule, reminding everyone about the potential dangers that lurked beyond our walls and fences.

The foraging parties continued to gather food from abandoned houses, but this was getting harder as the search radius increased and the pickings became more difficult to find, with only the occasional great discovery in the form of a fully stocked pantry.

Most of the people they encountered were in a desperate state, starving and becoming weaker by the day. In fact most of the food that was collected ended up being given to those poor souls.

It seemed wrong that our community, all with full stomachs, should only give a small amount to the starving people we came across and so, by unwritten agreement, we began to take food out on the foraging missions in order to give it to anyone we found who needed it. Logically and practically, it was the wrong thing to do. We couldn't help these people on a permanent basis, we just didn't have the supplies. We were probably only extending their suffering by giving them food. But when we came across a starving family, who had not eaten properly for weeks and who reminded us of old news footage of starving families in Africa, it was impossible not to offer them what help we could. We hoped that what little we could give them would give them the strength to start looking for food themselves, or maybe enable them to leave to find help elsewhere.

A few unfriendly or hostile groups were encountered. Some didn't want any help and told us in no uncertain terms to leave them alone, which we did.

We noted where they lived and Pete marked them on the large-scale map he had found of South Birmingham, as houses to avoid. Sometimes the foraging parties were attacked, usually by people wrongly thinking that we wanted to take what they had (in which case we tried to reassure them that this was not our intention to try to defuse the situation and prevent anyone getting hurt). The foraging parties did look quite intimidating, dressed in body armour and helmets and carrying weapons, so it was probably quite understandable that people were initially afraid of us and thought they needed to defend themselves.

Most of the time we were able to prevent any conflict from escalating and reassure them of our peaceful intentions.

On one occasion when I was with a foraging party, we came across another group out looking for food. They were all armed with a variety of weapons, including one shotgun and a few air rifles.

There were twelve of them, all men, and I had a bad feeling almost immediately. I quietly called Pete on the walkie-talkie and told him to send out as many armed reinforcements as he could spare. As we stood there, five of us and twelve of them, I noticed the man with the shotgun give a hand signal.

The rest of them started to spread out in an attempt to encircle us. I raised my MP5, aimed it at the man with the shotgun and shouted for the rest of them to stand still. As I raised my weapon, Allan's training kicked in and the rest of my group quickly responded by raising their weapons and running for the nearest cover. A stand-off ensued, with nobody wanting to make the next move. A tense few minutes went by until the reinforcements, pedalling madly, came round the corner behind them. The leader, realising he was now surrounded himself, and considerably out-gunned, decided to try to make a run for it. He turned and fired his gun at one of the cyclists, shouting to the rest of his men to attack. To my horror, I saw Bob fall from his bike screaming, having been hit by both barrels of the shotgun. We automatically opened fire. Caught in the crossfire between us, they didn't stand a chance. In a short while every one of them was either dead or dying on the road.

Ignoring them all we rushed over to Bob, who was writhing around in the road. His body armour had taken most of the blast, but quite a few pellets had hit him in one arm and both legs.

Jerry had given us all some basic First Aid training and we quickly cut away his sleeve and trouser legs to inspect the damage. He was in a lot of pain, but removing shotgun pellets was beyond our medical skills.

We needed to get him back to Jerry as a matter of urgency. I selected four people, escorted by three more, to start carrying Bob back home. I called Pete on the walkie-talkie, quickly explained what had happened and told him to get Jerry ready. Pete, thinking quickly as usual, said he would dispatch a few more people with a wheelbarrow to meet them so they could get Bob back as quickly as possible.

Although in a lot of pain, Bob managed to make us all chuckle by swearing repeatedly and telling the four who were carrying him that in about one hundred yards they would wish it was one of the skinny ones who'd been shot. One of them retorted that the skinny ones were harder to hit and the man had obviously chosen the largest and therefore easiest target to aim at. This prompted another torrent of abuse from Bob, directed at everyone around him, as the men carried him home.

Once they'd left, we looked around at all the dead bodies. Allan's training had clearly paid off. Not one of us had panicked and all the dead had been hit more than once, by well-aimed shots, either to the head or the trunk. I checked that everyone was OK, and they all agreed that they were going to attack us and therefore deserved their fate. They'd picked the wrong fight and paid the ultimate price.

Not wanting to leave a pile of rotting corpses in the road, we decided that, once again, burning the bodies would be the quickest and most hygienic way of disposing of them. We gathered up the weapons and searched their belongings for anything useful.

They'd been carrying a fair amount of food and we transferred this to our rucksacks. Everyone helped to build the pyre by gathering what timber we could from the surrounding houses and piling the bodies on top of it. I gave them a good soaking with petrol taken from the fuel tank of a nearby car and after setting it alight, we made our way home, not looking back once at the burning bodies we'd left behind.

Bob was being cared for by his wife, Jo, and Jerry when we got back. Jerry had removed all the pellets and stitched up the wounds. The patient was on good form, and under the influence of strong painkillers, was regaling all his visitors with stories of his bravery and the sacrifices he had made for the sake of the road.

The one good thing about the incident was that it reminded us all of the constant need for vigilance. We would only be safe if we worked and stayed together, protected by our defences.

CHAPTER TWENTY-FIVE

The weather was turning colder. Pete organised work parties to cut and gather wood, and gave the children the job of delivering logs to everyone's house on a daily basis. Some of us had log burners and this was the most efficient way to heat your house, so for those who didn't have one, we searched nearby properties, removed all the log burners we could find and fitted them for those who were without them. The installations might not have passed regulations, but they worked, and heated at least a few rooms in every house. The wood, having just been cut, was not seasoned, and therefore didn't burn as easily, but as long as the log burners were hot enough, they were fine. We knew the wood cutting would have to carry on all year round, to give us all a large enough supply of seasoned wood to last the following winter.

Mary was slowly recovering from the shock of Ian's death and decided that she wanted to contribute to our community.

She was a retired schoolteacher and, to all the children's dismay, they were made to attend her "school" every morning for a few hours, before being released to play and carry out the tasks that Pete kept finding for them. She worked hard on setting a curriculum that was appropriate for every child.

We were starting to operate as an independent little nation, amidst all the suffering and chaos that was happening around us. We had a form of government and a health service, providing free health and dental services, a school, a defence force and provisions, supplemented by the foragers searching properties for food, the fishermen who regularly caught fish from the lake and a team of hunters who, most days, provided us with ducks, geese, pigeons and squirrels.

Apart from Pete, who allocated the daily tasks at the morning meetings, and Jerry and Fiona, our doctor and dentist, not one of us had a specific job, but some of us were more proficient or enjoyed doing one task more than another.

Pete tried to be fair and keep us all happy by giving people jobs that they would enjoy, where possible. Our food situation was improving, as on a regular basis, more food was found per day than was consumed. We had fresh fish and meat most days and the only fresh ingredients missing from meals were vegetables. The vegetable patches we had between us couldn't supply us with anywhere near what we needed. Pete said that if we were still here in the spring we would need to start planning to plant more vegetables.

He told the foraging parties to check garden sheds for packets of seeds so that we could start building up a supply ready for planting. Becky had a sack of seed potatoes and she'd already planted most of them in cleared flower beds. It was not the best time to plant them, but if the weather was favourable, they could provide us with an early harvest.

We discovered another food source while working in the back gardens, which were all now connected.

I noticed Harriet, a neighbour's little girl, feeding her rabbits in their hutch. To pass the time, I went to have a chat with her and ask how she was getting on. I asked her the names of her rabbits, (they all had girls' names), and then it hit me. Rabbits breed like rabbits! If we could find some male rabbits, then pretty soon we would have plenty of them, and rabbit stew tasted pretty good. A quick check revealed that Russell's son, Oliver, had a rabbit called Butch which they thought was male. After promising Harriet and Oliver that we wouldn't eat their pets, we put Butch out to stud with the lady rabbits and eagerly waited to see if he would live up to his name.

We tied ribbons around the necks of the two pets, so that in the event of a population explosion, we could identify them and so avoid putting the wrong rabbit in the pot.

My chickens were still providing eggs every day, but not nearly enough for everyone, so we were on the lookout for a cockerel so that we could start getting fertilized eggs.

Then we would start building up the population to provide more eggs, and eventually chickens, to eat.

The rabbits, vegetable gardens and, hopefully, the chickens (once a cockerel was found), were all longer-term projects. It was a good psychological boost for all of us to think that we were planning for the future and not just finding food for the next meal.

In the meantime, Allan and Michelle were becoming close friends. He made a habit of "just popping in", to see if she was doing well and needed anything. They spent a lot of their spare time talking quietly in a corner or walking around outside. You could tell that they were attracted to each other, but Allan knew what she had been through and respected the fact that it would be a long time before she was ready for an intimate relationship. They were both content to be friends and get to know each other. We were all very happy for him, as everyone on the road had family or friends they had known for years around them, and at times, he must have felt like an outsider.

But it didn't stop me or some of the others from taking the mickey out of him, in a juvenile way, when the women were out of earshot.

Pete had held back from giving Michelle, Kim or Mandy jobs to do yet, as we all wanted to give them time to recover and we had enough people to get all the daily chores and tasks done.

But in the end they told us that they wanted to contribute and were bored with sitting around all day. Michelle had worked as a PA to the boss of a large firm of accountants in the city, so Pete told her that when she was ready, she could help him in his role as community leader. He was always producing lists and rotas, so someone with Michelle's administrative expertise would be a real help to him. Kim had been a massage therapist and when she felt able to, Pete arranged for her to be Jerry's medical assistant. They set up a therapy room, where she could offer massage therapy to alleviate the aching backs and muscles we were all getting from the unaccustomed physical exercise.

Mandy had been a teaching assistant in a local primary school and settled gladly into helping Mary in the schoolroom. Becky joked that she wasn't happy about the idea of me receiving a massage from an attractive twenty-one-year-old, so I responded by complaining about my aching back and muscles and the fact that I couldn't wait for Kim to relieve me of the constant pain I was in. After all, I grinned, if only my wife would give me a massage every night I wouldn't feel the need to use her!

Russell revealed his latest invention. He had designed a water filtration system which, he assured us, would enable the stream water, once it had passed through it, to be drunk without boiling. I'd allowed him to take apart one of the filters for my water filtering system and he'd cleverly reverse engineered it and reproduced it on a bigger scale. Boiling enough water for drinking was a tedious chore and Russ's oven was kept going virtually all day, boiling pots of water to provide us all with enough to drink.

This created a lot of work, as a couple of people had to stand there and watch water boil all day, and it used up a great deal of wood for fuel, which took a lot of labour to provide. He was also working on a pump, with a system of pipes constructed from garden hoses joined together, to get the water from the stream up to the road, without the tedious and back-breaking work of carrying it up in buckets. Who would have thought, that in 2014, we would all be so excited about the imminent arrival of running water on the street?

CHAPTER TWENTY-SIX

A couple of times a week now we had people, either as individuals, or in groups, approaching our barricades and begging for help. It appeared that even those who'd had plenty of food stored at home, or had had the foresight, when the power went out, to gather as much as they could, were starting to run low or had run out completely. After a full community meeting, we agreed on a procedure to follow. If they claimed that they were just passing by and were trying to get somewhere, we would offer them help. We would give them a hot meal and water, and Jerry would offer what medical assistance he could. If they lived locally, we would question them about how they had survived so long and why we had not come across them on our foraging trips which, by this time, had covered most of the immediate surrounding area.

If they seemed genuine, and we were in agreement, we would offer them a meal and the chance to join in our next foraging expedition, and they would be allowed to share in what we found. We wouldn't allow them into our compound, as we didn't want them to see the setup we had and we wanted to avoid the possibility of their refusing to leave, and having to eject them by force. Allan insisted on this, because he feared that that there might be spies from other groups of survivors, who just wanted to check us out and look for weak points in our defences.

Most people were grateful for the help we offered and in some cases, were reduced to tears by our kindness. Some wanted us to give them food, as if it was their right to receive free handouts in return for no effort on their part.

They became aggressive, telling us that we had to give them something, or we would regret it. We had all worked incredibly hard to get the food we had and to ensure the safety of our community, so in those cases we would offer them no help at all.

The food was ours to give out and if they weren't prepared to show the least bit of gratitude or humility, we wanted nothing to do with them. They were on their own.

This did of course lead to confrontations, but Allan had trained us all well and we were perfectly capable of getting them to leave. Unfortunately, some of them still thought they had the right to take what we had and the outcome was wearily predictable. They would eventually leave after a lot of persuasion by us and threats from them. At some point during the next few nights they would return and attempt to break in, either by sneaking up to the barricades on the road, or attempting to scale the fences in the back gardens. After a few attempts, we were prepared for this and Allan increased the patrols and people on the barricades for a few nights following each confrontation.

Most were unable to get close to the barricades without being spotted. A few shots over their heads usually scared them off for good. It was the same with the fences in the back gardens.

Allan and I had designed them so that they were virtually impossible for someone to climb over, without becoming caught in the barbed wire or injured on the nails that protruded from everywhere along the fence. They normally left after a fruity exchange of words through the fence and were never seen again. Some were more persistent and tried to use ladders to scale the fences or barricades.

It was not difficult to spot them, because it was pitch black at night and they either had to use torches to find their way in, or the tin can alarms all along the fence alerted us to their attempts before they'd managed to scale it. If they did succeed in breaching our perimeter, then for the safety of everyone, we were forced to treat them as a serious threat and adopted a "shoot first, ask questions later" policy. They could have accepted our offer of help, but they chose not to and were trying to take what we had by force. We had no sympathy for them if they were killed as a result of their folly. Allan kept a record of every incident and, if possible, the identities of the people we'd had to kill. If in the future someone tried to hold us accountable for our actions, we hoped Allan's record of the events would prove that we'd done the best we could.

From speaking to the people who approached the barricades, and the others we encountered on our foraging trips, we were steadily building up a picture of what was happening to our once great city of Birmingham. By our calculations, in the areas we had covered, aside from our group, no more than one hundred people were still alive. Whole streets had nothing but empty abandoned houses, or houses with corpses in them. Doing a rough tally of the corpses we found, hundreds of thousands of people must have fled the city, hoping to find either government-run refugee camps, if they existed, or at least food in the countryside. If this scenario had been repeated all over the country, swarms of people must had spread out from the cities to find food. What the conditions must now be like, or how many of them had even survived, didn't bear thinking about.

We didn't know exactly how many people had lived in the area before the event, but there must easily have been two hundred thousand and now we only knew of one hundred people, plus our group of fifty-five, who were still alive.

People who were escaping the city and had approached us for help, had reported that other areas of the city were just as empty. Most of it had been abandoned.

Occasionally we'd come across signs of cannibalism on our trips. We found bones that were definitely human, near abandoned campfires, and rotting corpses with missing limbs, which looked as if they had been removed with a saw or knife. None of us really talked about this, but the fact that people had been desperate enough to eat a fellow human being was a grim reminder of what you might be reduced to in order to survive. I fervently hoped I'd never be faced with such a decision.

It was now the middle of December and becoming much colder, with a sharp frost most nights. Even with the log burners going full time it was hard to keep warm in the houses, so I started to dispense the coal I'd bought before the event. Coal burns much hotter and for longer than logs, so it helped to keep the cold at bay. As I only had a limited amount, Pete rationed it and distributed it when it looked as if it was going to be a particularly cold night. We were conscious that January was normally the coldest month and wanted to conserve as much of it as possible for then. We'd found some portable gas heaters and these were given to the older members of the community so that, using the gas bottles I had, they could be made more comfortable.

The cooking marquee had been extended and fully enclosed, using a wooden frame and tarpaulins, and even on the coldest day the Beast became a focal point, as we gathered round it to absorb the warmth radiating from it, and tried not to get in the way of the cooks.

CHAPTER TWENTY-SEVEN

I was on a foraging trip just before Christmas. The parties were now often as large as twenty people, as most of the survivors we met were keen to join us in the continual search for food. Pete called me on the walkie-talkie and asked me to return urgently. He assured me that nothing bad had happened, but I needed to get back straightaway. Luckily, we hadn't long started the trip so I was only a fifteen-minute jog away from home. As I returned, out of breath from the run, I was met by an incredible sight. My sister Jane, her husband Michael and her children were sitting at my kitchen table, filthy, on the edge of exhaustion and starvation, but alive. I stood for a moment, not believing what I was seeing. Jane stood up, rushed over to me and we hugged each other, tears streaming down our cheeks. "How are you here?"

I asked, "Where have you been all this time?" I had so many questions and in my excitement, I just kept asking them, not giving my sister or Michael a chance to reply. Becky gently told me to calm down and give Jane a chance to speak.

This is their story.

They had turned up at the campsite in the middle of the Friday morning on the day of the event. The campsite was in a remote part of the country on the English/Welsh border, about eighty miles from Birmingham. By the time they'd set up their tents, most of their friends from school had arrived and they were all busy helping each other set up the camp. They'd only realised that something had happened when another friend turned up on foot, saying that his car had broken down about a mile down the road.

He wanted someone to give him a lift back, so that he could get the rest of the family to the campsite and set up while he waited for the recovery services to arrive. He asked to borrow a mobile phone as his was strangely out of battery.

It was only when everybody had taken out their own phones, and found that they weren't working either, and then discovered that nobody's car would start, that Jane had remembered my phone call of a few days before.

She apologised to me at this point for not taking my warning seriously.

When she'd told them all what I had told her nobody had believed her. One of her friends had even declared himself to be an expert on the subject, and had categorically stated that any event would only be localised, if it had happened at all. If they just stayed put and enjoyed the weekend, everything would be put right by Monday.

Over the course of the day, more weary people had arrived at the campsite, having abandoned their now useless cars and walked the rest of the way. The farmer had been very understanding and had apologised that, as all his vehicles were out of order, he couldn't offer any help in that way, but he did have some spare camping equipment which he gave out to those who turned up without.

In spite of everything they'd all had a great weekend and hadn't really given any of it much more thought until the Sunday, when they'd realised that as their mobile phones still weren't working, they weren't going to be able to call the recovery services. They'd gone to see the farmer, who explained that even his land line wasn't working and he'd had no electricity since Friday lunchtime. They were stuck on the side of a Welsh mountain and there was no easy way for any of them to get home.

"But what about the bikes I made you promise to take with you?" I asked. She looked at me, on the verge of tears again, saying,

"I'm sorry, I only said that to keep you happy. We didn't have enough room to put them on the car because we had our roof box, and we'd got so much stuff to take with us." I was about to say something else, but noticed the warning look Becky was giving me over their heads. I clamped my mouth shut and listened to the rest of their story.

The mood at the campsite had changed, and tempers had begun to fray, when people realised that they stood no chance of getting to work on Monday. They'd had no choice but to wait another day and see what happened. On Monday the farmer reported that his son had cycled the ten miles to the nearest village and found that everything was the same there. About half of the families decided to walk home and left, but Jane and the rest decided to wait another day or so, instead of attempting the long gruelling walk home. They ended up staying at the farm for over two weeks. By then, the farmer's son had cycled to all the nearest towns in the area and found terrible conditions, with people fighting over whatever food was left, so they all decided to stay rather than risk the walk home. The farm was very isolated, up a long track, and quite a distance away from the next house, so the farmer locked the gate at the bottom of the drive and removed all the signs advertising its presence, in the hope that they would avoid any trouble that might come their way. It worked, because in all the time they were there nobody else found them.

The farmer had been very generous and had given everyone food to eat from the small abattoir and meat processing business he ran from his farm, supplying bacon, sausages and other meat products to local farm shops.

After about two weeks though, things had changed.

He'd stopped giving out food, saying that he only had enough now for himself and his family. He was apologetic, but he needed to look after his family because, by now, everybody had realised that no help was coming. He had given them all enough supplies to last a few days and advised them all to try to make it home.

They had been left with no option but to leave, if not for home, then at least somewhere that they could get help.

They had left as a group, but after walking for a couple of hours, they had been attacked by a large group of armed men who had tried to take everything they were carrying.

Two of the men had been killed when they'd tried to resist. Terrified, they'd all split up and run in any direction they could to escape.

My sister, Michael and their children and two other families, had spent two terrible weeks, slowly making their way home, living off any food they could find growing in the fields and hedgerows, and avoiding any roads or villages. Often they were forced to hide from gangs roaming the countryside, and they came across many houses that had been ransacked and the occupants murdered. On one occasion they'd witnessed, from a distance, a gun battle between two gangs. Not stopping to find out the cause, they'd headed in the opposite direction as quickly as they could.

Eventually, starving and suffering from diarrhoea from drinking untreated stream water, they came across an army roadblock just outside Kidderminster, twenty miles from Birmingham.

The armed forces had set up a refugee camp and were attempting to feed and control the growing number of people who were arriving from the city on a daily basis.

Grateful, and believing that they were now safe, they had entered the camp.

A huge area had been surrounded by a high fence and a tented village had been erected inside. Conditions had been appalling in the camp, but initially at least, there had been basic washing facilities and medical care and two meals a day. Thousands more people had arrived on a daily basis and the camp had soon become overcrowded. The toilet and washing facilities had been unable to cope and had overflowed. The army was doing its best, but there were just too many people to cope with. The information the soldiers had given them had been sketchy at best, or non-existent and there was no way of contacting anybody in charge to find out what was going on. At meal times the portions were becoming smaller and smaller and sometimes no food was given out at all. The army spokesman had assured them that they were waiting for supplies to arrive. Nobody was allowed to leave the camp. They were told that it was safer for them to stay and order gradually broke down.

There were not enough beds or blankets to go around and fights over sleeping spaces became commonplace. Jane and Michael were desperate to leave, but were terrified to, after their experiences on their journey. The soldiers, unable to keep the peace inside the camp, had retreated to the other side of the fence. Michael talked to a few of them to try to get information. They knew very little other than the fact that quite a few of these camps had been set up around the country, and conditions were bad there too.

Not one of the soldiers had received any news about their own families, and their rations had also been cut due to the supplies not being delivered. The camp descended into chaos.

About three days before, they had announced that there would no meals that day due to supply problems.

A serious riot had been started by a large group of troublemakers, who been terrorising the rest of the camp's inhabitants since the soldiers had retreated behind the fences. The fences had been rushed by the angry mob and the main gate had broken under the sheer weight of numbers. A few soldiers had been attacked and the other soldiers, either in panic or desperation to help their mates, had opened fire. The rioters had snatched up the weapons from the soldiers they'd already overcome, and fired back. In the ensuing madness the soldiers had opened up with everything they had.

After about thirty seconds, the firing had ceased and the soldiers had regained control, but hundreds had been killed or wounded. In the panic to get away from the firing, many more had been crushed or trampled to death. As soon as the mood had turned ugly following the announcement about the food, Jane and Michael had taken the children as far away from the trouble as possible, sheltering with hundreds of other families who'd had the same idea at the far edge of the camp.

After it was all over and the rioters had been killed or run away, the army had made a sweep of the camp and gathered up all the remaining occupants. The senior officer, a Captain, addressed the remaining refugees. He looked pale and shocked, but he stoutly defended the actions of his soldiers, stating that they had acted in self-defence and under the standing orders he had issued.

He deeply regretted the loss of life. He was aware that many of the dead had been innocent and was sorry that he had been unable to protect them.

The situation they'd all found themselves in was unique and, as he had not heard from his superiors at all for two days and did not think that they were going to receive any more supplies, the only option remaining to him, was to close the camp and attempt to return to his barracks. They would have to travel on foot, as any working vehicle he had, had been requisitioned for use by other units.

He gave the camp occupants two options: they could either return to the barracks with the soldiers, where they would continue to try to protect them and share what supplies were available, or they could leave and go where they chose. He had enough MREs to give at least a few meals to everybody who wanted to leave, but then they would be on their own and they'd have to fend for themselves. He warned that from the few reports he had received, the whole country appeared to be in chaos, with the government having ceased to exist and military and police units unable to cope with the gangs roaming wild and leaving death and destruction in their wake. All the units he'd had contact with were basically operating independently, as the army leaders had either been overrun or had disappeared.

Jane and Michael had decided to leave and head for home.

The bleak picture painted by the captain, and everything they had witnessed on their journey so far, had made them realise that he couldn't guarantee their safety and in any case, how long would the supplies he claimed to have back at the barracks last? It was too risky to put their safety in his hands and they knew that they had a lot of food at home, if it was still there.

They had passed the end of our road on the last leg of their journey and seeing the barricade of cars, had stopped to see if we were still there.

My neighbours knew my sister, so they'd immediately let them through the barricade, taken them to my house and asked Pete to call me on the walkie-talkie.

While they were eating their first decent meal for weeks, I filled them in on what had happened locally and what we had been doing to survive. I explained that their house had been ransacked, but that the food stored in the cellar was still there, (every time I had passed the house I'd given it a quick check over and the cellar door was still locked).

I don't know why I hadn't taken the food yet; maybe I'd sensed that she was OK and would need it someday. Jane confirmed that she'd had her monthly shop delivered just before they'd left, but a few weeks before she'd also done a big shop at Costco where, two or three times a year, she'd stocked up on things like rice, pasta and tinned tomatoes, because it saved her the hassle of getting them on the monthly shop and it worked out much cheaper. I jokingly accused her of being a secret prepper. She denied it, saying that she was just a lazy shopper.

She already knew that Michelle was living with us, as they'd met before I'd arrived, but I didn't tell Jane what she had been through. That would be Michelle's story to tell in her own words.

Of course I insisted that they stay with us. The house would be very crowded, with every bedroom now occupied, but the cousins could bunk up together and Jane and Michael could have the last spare room to themselves.

In the future Michelle, Kim or Mandy might decide to move to another house, but that would be their decision and I wasn't going to ask them to leave. I'd already told them that they would be welcome for as long as they wanted to stay.

I told Pete that I was going to take the rest of the day off to spend it with my family and to start getting them used to our new communal way of living. I suspected that after what they'd been through, it would be bliss.

CHAPTER TWENTY-EIGHT

In the evening, once my sister and her family had all had showers to wash the grime off, and got the kids settled down to sleep, all the nine adults in the house sat in the lounge, relaxing and enjoying a couple of specially released bottles of wine in celebration of the new arrivals. The log burner blazed and Jane and Michael went back over their experiences with us. As soon as Michael mentioned that the army officers had been unable to contact their superiors, Jerry sat up straight, made a strange noise and looked pained. All conversation stopped as we wondered what was wrong with him.

"The radio my brother gave us! We haven't even tried to turn it on since we looked at it at my house. He could have been trying to contact me." As everybody else, with the exception of Fiona, was looking a little confused, I explained about the military radio in the crate, and the weapons that Jerry's brother, Colonel Moore, had sent him.

I told them that we'd tried to switch it on, but hadn't been able to get it to work, so we'd put it back in the crate, and had forgotten all about it.

Jerry brought it into the room along with the instructions. Being men, we didn't bother with those and just turned it on and started to push buttons and twiddle knobs to see what would happen.

All we got was static. Becky and Fiona, who had picked up the discarded instructions and had been reading them for a few minutes, told us to move our ignorant backsides out of the way and let the ones who had actually read the instructions have a go.

Jerry and I returned to our seats somewhat sulkily. After a few minutes of nothing but static, with both of the girls referring to the manual and pressing another button or turning a dial, they actually got something.

It was faint at first, and very garbled, so you couldn't understand what was being said, but it was definitely a voice. It kept fading in and out. No matter what they did, they couldn't get it to sound any clearer.

"We need to get Russ in on this, he knows about these things." I said. I stood up and was about to run over to his house and wake him up, but Becky said,

"Leave it till the morning, we're all shattered. Look at Jane and Michael. They can hardly keep their eyes open. Jo isn't going to thank you for waking them all up at this hour."

I started to protest so she said sharply, "It's been sitting in that bloody crate for over a month because you both forgot about it, one more night isn't going to make a difference, now let's all go to bed."

Once again I knew when I'd lost, so with a final grunt of disagreement, I sat down and finished my drink. We all said our good nights and went to bed.

In the morning Jerry and I were up and dressed earlier than usual. Picking up the radio, we walked over to Russ's house, knocked quickly, and walked straight in. We didn't lock our front doors in the road now.

With so many people living in each house and people coming and going, changing guard shifts throughout the night, it wasn't practical to do it. They could all be locked and barred quickly from the inside in the event of an emergency, though.

Russ was already up, sitting at his kitchen table, drawing out plans for another one of his inventions. He looked up in surprise at our early entry. He looked even more surprised when he saw what Jerry was carrying.

"Where the bloody hell did you get that beauty from?" he asked. Jerry and I told him the story and how we'd forgotten all about it. In response to the look of disapproval he gave us, when we admitted to having forgotten it, I hurriedly explained that I'd been more interested in showing Jerry how the guns worked at the time, so I hadn't given the radio much thought. And what with everything that had happened since, somehow I hadn't really thought about it again until Jerry had remembered last night.

Russ, by now, had removed it from Jerry's grip and was virtually drooling over it. "I read about these, it's the latest military radio. The article said it's full of top-secret stuff, which they couldn't go into, but it'll provide a massive upgrade for the military, and will eliminate all the communication issues they've been having with the old equipment they've been using until now."

"But can you get it to work?" I asked, impatiently.

"It'd be a lot easier with some sort of manual," he replied. Grinning, I reached into the pocket of my coat and dropped the instruction manual on the table in front of him. He didn't even look up at us, saying, "Both of you idiots, out! Give me an hour or so and I'll come and find you."

We went back to the house and helped get the children up. Then Becky and I showed my sister and her family around our community, starting with the food tent first where, by now, most people who were not on duty were gathering.

Everybody knew about their arrival and was interested in what was happening out there, so after breakfast, Pete, who had been over to see them the day before and was up to date with everything, gave a résumé of what had happened to them, and what we had learned about what was going on in the outside world.

Neither Pete nor anyone else knew about the radio yet. I decided not to tell them and get their hopes up, until we knew that Russ could get it working.

While we were showing my sister around all the perimeter fences and everything else we had done to improve our safety, Pete allocated the day's duties. He had already told me I was on hunting duties today, which would enable me to stay close to home and be there for my family should they need me. I'd already thanked him for his thoughtfulness and promised I'd join the rest of the hunters as soon as I could. I enjoyed the hunting days more than any other.

We'd constructed hides around the back gardens and in the park and set out decoys to attract ducks, geese and pigeons. Food had been laid out to attract squirrels, but as the weather was getting colder, they were mostly snuggled in their dreys and weren't around as much. Most days we managed to decoy in a flight of ducks or geese to the lake, or pigeons on to the grass and, depending on the prey, we would use either the air rifles or shotguns. The fishermen always complained, saying that the noise stopped the fish from biting, but the daily catch didn't seem to be affected if a shot was fired or not. The banter between both groups was always good humoured.

I explained all this to Jane and Michael as I gave them the tour, and told them how much food we had collected and stored, and about the other projects we were working on, such as the rabbit breeding programme, which we hoped would help to extend our food supplies.

We agreed that as soon as possible, we would go and collect the food from their house and that it would all be added to the community supply. Jerry and I already had enough food stored separately at my house, and also in Jerry's cellar to last us for a long time if need be. I always checked on Jerry's cellar when we passed, and remained confident that it was unlikely to be found behind the hidden doorway unless you knew it was there. It would therefore be selfish for us to keep any of it. As they were joining the community, if they could start with a large donation of food, then although there were no disagreements as yet, and we were all working well together while we had plenty of food, it might prevent any future conflict, if food did become scarce at any time.

CHAPTER TWENTY-NINE

I spotted Russ making his way hurriedly over to us, so I left Becky to continue the tour. He'd managed to work out most of the features on the radio and was confident that he could send and receive on it, if we managed to find anyone out there.

"The problem is, all I get is static at the moment, so I think we might be out of range. We need to go to the highest point in the area and see if that extends the range. If you want to come with me, I think we should climb the church steeple to the belfry and see if it works up there." He was pointing at the church on the next road over.

"OK," I said, "I'll go and tell Pete you need me to help you with something and we'll give it a go."

I went to speak to Pete. He could tell that we were up to something, but he trusted us, so he gave us a knowing look and went back to his lists and rotas.

He crossed me off the hunting rota, and added Jerry and me to the list of the people working on the outside of the perimeter. He maintained these lists constantly, so that he always knew at a glance where everyone would be. I grabbed my tool bag, as we hadn't ventured into the church before. We'd emptied the church hall of all sorts of useful items, but we'd all felt that it was wrong to take anything from the church itself and had left it alone. Out of habit, we both carried our MP5s with us.

Even though we knew that the chance of encountering anyone was now slim, we had a strict rule that if anyone left the perimeter, at least one person should be armed. The radio came with shoulder straps, so Jerry carried it while I lugged the heavy tool bag.

I recalled from previous visits to the church that the belfry entrance was a small door on the side of the steeple. It was a heavy oak door and it took me some effort with my crowbar before I was able to break the lock and gain access.

When we reached the belfry, after climbing the tight spiral stairs, we noticed a ladder leading to a trap door that gave access on to the walkway around the top of the steeple, where the spire began.

The view up there was incredible. You could see most of South Birmingham, and the city looked strangely normal from this height. Looking more closely, you could see the burnt-out houses and abandoned cars littering the road, but in the distance over the rooftops, it all looked as if nothing had happened at all.

"We should have used this as a regular look-out post ages ago," I said.

"It would have been the best way to see what was going on. Oh well, too late to worry about that now. I'll mention it to Pete when we get back."

Russ was busy setting up the radio and was oblivious to the view. I left him to it as I picked out all the landmarks I could see, wishing I'd brought my binoculars with me. Russ looked up and said, "I've just set it to scan for frequencies with any voice traffic on them."

I stopped my inspection of the Birmingham skyline and crouched down next to the radio. Suddenly the radio broadcast loud and clear:

"Team one reporting. Main gate inspected and all secure, continuing perimeter check." We looked at each other in amazement.

"Well done, mate!" I said, slapping him on the back. "Now what?"

"I suppose I should try and contact them and see what happens," said Russ. He picked up the handset and spoke, "Hello, can anybody hear me? We are a group of survivors. Is there anybody who can tell us what is going on? I repeat, we are a group of survivors who have formed a small community to help each other. We would like some news about what is happening out there. Over." We looked at each other expectantly, but nobody answered. We waited for five minutes, then the radio sprang to life.

"Unidentified caller, identify yourself immediately." It was a very terse reply. I nodded at Russ to carry on.

"I repeat. We are a group who have formed a small community and are managing to survive. We want to know if there is anybody in control out there." The reply came back immediately.

"This is a secure frequency. How and why are you using this to contact us?" I took the handset from Russ and replied.

"We were given the radio before the EMP hit. Look, we've been surviving on our own since the event, and have been attacked on many occasions and been forced to defend ourselves. We haven't seen or heard from anyone in authority since it happened. Hundreds of thousands must already have died of starvation, or have been killed by the gangs roaming wild. And you're asking me why I'm contacting you?"

"Hold on," came the brief reply. A few seconds later the radio burst into life again.

"This is Captain Hardy. How can I help you?"

I handed the handset back to Russ so that he could continue. "Captain Hardy, hello. My name is Russ. Am I speaking to the man in charge?"

"Hello Russ. Let me put it this way, you are speaking to the most in charge person you are going to talk to until you can convince me otherwise. Can you tell me about yourselves and how you and your group are doing? Please tell us everything. We've had little or no news for weeks, apart from occasional contact with other units." Russ looked at me and said, "Do you want to do this?" I nodded and took the handset back.

I told Captain Hardy the basics of our story, from when I first became aware of what was going to happen, to the initial attacks. I explained how we'd built our fences for protection and described some of the things we'd done to keep us all safe.

I didn't say where we'd got the radio from, because I didn't want to land Jerry's brother in trouble, but I told him how the return of my sister, and hearing her story, had reminded us about the forgotten radio, which was how we were able to talk to him now. When I'd finished, he was silent for a while and politely asked us to hold on as he was passing us on to someone else.

"This is Colonel Moore speaking, who am I talking to?" I started to smile.

"Hello, my name is Tom. Do you happen to have a brother called Jerry?"

END OF BOOK 1

Printed in Great Britain
by Amazon